BACK TO YOU
TURNING TIDES SERIES BOOK 1

CARLY GRANT

Copyright © 2021 by Carly Grant

All rights reserved.

No part of this book may be reproduced, duplicated, or transmitted in any form or by any electronic or mechanical means, including information storage and retrieval systems without written permission of the author, except for the use of brief quotations in a book review.

This book is a work of fiction. Unless otherwise indicated, all of the names, characters, businesses, places, events and incidents in this book are either the product of the author's imagination or used in a fictitious manner. Any resemblance to persons, living or dead, or places, events or locations is purely coincidental.

BACK TO YOU

A Turning Tides Novel

Welcome to Crestpoint Beach, where warm sands and sea breezes bring sweet second chances, renewed family ties, and the comfort of coming home.

Heartbroken and lost. That's how Annie Collins left small-town Crestpoint Beach when she was eighteen and an aspiring interior designer. And that's how she returns years later, starting over as a widow at thirty-five.

Coming home to help care for her aging father while she sorts out her life, Annie moves into her grandparents' old beach house. The big, beautiful home needs a little TLC, but Annie has the support of her free-spirited younger sister, Hannah, who dreams of turning the beach house into a B&B together. If only repairing Annie's wounded heart were that easy.

Complicating things even more, her high school heartbreak, Noah Davis, still lives in Crestpoint Beach. Now the town's favorite science teacher, recently divorced single dad Noah is the same handsome, charming man he was back then. Soon, that charm draws Annie back into his life with his teenage daughter, Lainey. Noah walked away from Annie once; will he stand by her this time, even when his ex-wife would like nothing better than to split them apart?

Back to You is a clean contemporary romance. Book 1 of the Turning Tides B&B series.

Watch for Book 2, **Meant to Be**, coming March 17, 2021.

CHAPTER 1

You can never go home again. That's what people say, anyway.

After going from newlywed to widow all in the space of about a year, home was the only place Annie Collins wanted to be. So, today she had made the eleven-hour drive from Dallas to her small hometown of Crestpoint Beach on the Gulf Coast of Florida.

She hadn't been back since she graduated high school and left to attend college in Texas on a full scholarship. She'd gone there to build a career in interior design, something she loved. If she was being honest with herself, she'd also left Crestpoint Beach because she thought the time and distance might help heal the broken heart she'd been nursing since the night of her senior prom.

That wound was ancient history, or so she wanted to think.

Either way, she was returning home with another ache in her heart. Nine months ago, her husband, Derek Collins, had been killed in a motorcycle accident. They had only been married for half a year when it happened. Most days the thought of him being gone still came as a painful shock.

After working for ten years at a large interior design firm in Dallas, Annie had been wooed away by the handsome, talented architect to join his startup as his partner. They worked well together and Derek's fast-paced life was a fun distraction for Annie, who'd always been a little too driven and focused on her career. He swept her off her feet, even though she hadn't been looking for a serious relationship. Before Derek, she'd barely even dated, focusing on her career instead.

Still, it took him two years to persuade her to marry him. Annie wasn't sure why she'd held out for so long. She finally said yes, then six months after they eloped, he was gone.

Without him to head their small company, she had little choice but to close it down. The house they'd been building together only reminded her of her loss, so she'd put the big two-story brick home on the market even though the sale had barely paid off the mortgage. Derek's family and the handful of friends she'd made in Dallas had promised to keep in touch, but she knew the distance from all of them probably meant goodbye.

She even had to leave Derek behind in his family's graveyard plot. All she had left was the $100,000 life insurance check she'd received upon his passing. She couldn't bear to cash it. Depositing the money seemed too final of a step. It made his death too real, and she didn't feel ready to let go of him completely yet.

Annie pushed away her sad thoughts as she rolled through quaint, downtown Crestpoint Beach to the scattering of residential streets where her father, Frank Taylor, lived. Although the family also owned a large beach house right on the sand, the three-story Victorian had too many steps for her father's arthritic knees and hips, so it had been sitting empty most of the time since Grandpa Joe and Grandma Betsy passed away.

Frank, a widower since Annie was eight years old, lived with Annie's younger sister, Hannah, in the same house where he'd raised his two girls as a single father after the loss of their mother, Ginny, to cancer when she was just thirty-three. Hannah had been looking after their dad since Annie left home, but now it was time for Annie to pitch in, too.

She parked her Corolla in the short driveway outside the cute white three-bedroom bungalow. Pushing her car door open, she tentatively stepped out and took a fortifying breath. A soft breeze brushed against her cheek, prompting her to pause and look at the small neighborhood that had seen generations of families come and go over the years. The beach was a few streets over, which was the heart of the town and its three thousand year-round residents. Admittedly, Annie had missed it.

After grabbing her suitcase and a duffel bag from the backseat of the car, Annie headed to the house. The cheery jingle of a handcrafted wind chime with painted fan scallops and calico clam shells met her as she reached the front door. It seemed Hannah was still keeping busy with her seashell art. With a faint smile, Annie walked into the house, her black flats meeting the weathered wooden floor of the small foyer.

"Hello?" She called out softly. She only had to walk a few steps forward to enter the living room, immediately spotting her father in his favorite beige leather recliner that he'd had since she was a little girl. As usual, he was working on the crossword puzzle in the town's daily newspaper, his eyes narrowed in concentration behind his black-framed reading glasses. He looked up at her, a sympathetic smile crossing his lips.

"Welcome home, kiddo." With a grin, he slowly folded the newspaper up and placed it on a nearby side table.

Before Annie could reply, Hannah strode in through the swinging kitchen door with a plate of fried catfish and coleslaw in her hand.

"Okay, Dad, dinner is served. I went light on the batter for you and—Annie!" Hannah gasped at the sight of her older sister, her body jerking back so fast the plate slipped out of her hand and splattered its contents all over the wooden living room floor.

"Oh, no!" Annie gaped at the mess. She began to move forward to help clean up, but she was practically tackled by her sister instead. Hannah stepped past the spilled food and grabbed her in a bear hug.

"I...can't...breathe!" Annie managed to say through happy laughter as Hannah squeezed her tightly. She rubbed Hannah's back, her hand sifting under her sister's long blonde hair.

They differed slightly in appearance. Annie, with her shoulder-length, straight blonde hair, was taller and less curvy, while Hannah had their mother's petite, sylph-like figure and beachy mermaid curls. What they did share was their blue eyes, which matched their father's.

"I'm so happy you're finally here," Hannah exclaimed as she pulled away to beam at her. "It feels like forever since we've seen you!"

"It's been a while. I'm sorry, that's my fault," Annie admitted. She should've visited home more often, but work and her life in Dallas had claimed a lot of her time. Too much. She didn't realize how badly she'd needed her family until now.

"No, we get it. You and Derek were busy with the company and the new house..." Hannah waved off Annie's concern, a sad smile crossing her lips. "You don't have to apologize for anything."

"We're really sorry about Derek, honey," Frank murmured as he stood and shuffled over to sweep Annie into a gentle embrace. All the years he worked as a lighthouse keeper had taken a toll on him; pain and soreness were evident in his every step.

Annie suspected his arthritis was getting worse, adding another thing for her to worry about. She had just lost her husband. She didn't want to see her father suffer. She was just glad he was retired and could take it easy now.

"My main concern right now is you," Annie told him. She glanced at Hannah. "And I've missed my little sister, too."

"We're both just glad you're here now." Frank said, letting her go. "So, relax and get comfortable, okay?"

Annie nodded, murmuring a quiet thank you. She needed this. Her world had been turned upside down, filling her with grief. She was afraid of drowning in it, and coming home was her chance to find her center again.

"I'm going to go put my stuff down and help you clean up, Hannah. I'm sorry about Dad's dinner."

Hannah waved off her apology. "Don't worry, I've got it. Go get settled."

Annie tugged her luggage down a short hallway leading to the other bedrooms and a bathroom. At the end of the hall to her left was her childhood bedroom, which, to her amazement, looked exactly as it did when she'd left home at eighteen.

The purple sheets and comforter of her twin-size bed were faded to lavender now, but instantly brought her back to her high school years. The vanity next to her dresser still had a box full of old makeup near the mirror. She couldn't count how many old decorating sketches and posters of pop singers and handsome movie stars still hung, curled and sun-bleached on the walls. It was the haven of a teenager with extraordinary passions and big dreams. Now, she was a widow without a shred of inspiration for her future.

Annie placed her suitcase on her bed and opened it, pulling out a few clothes to hang in the closet. She carried a few shirts over and opened the small door, finding a small collection of empty hangers and a forgotten box of her mementos on the floor. There was no lid, so she could see right in to the mix of old dolls, a few diaries, and well-used art supplies.

Her heart sank at the sight of the dolls, with their tangled hair and mismatched clothing. She loved those dolls. She would have loved for her own daughter to play with them, but that hadn't been in the cards.

There was a time when she'd dreamed of having kids and a family of her own. She longed for the chance to be the mother she never got to have as a child. How many hours did she lie on her bed, staring up at the glow-in-the-dark stars glued to the ceiling while she imagined what her future would look like?

Despite her big career dreams, she had also hoped to make memories with a daughter who looked like her, and a son with a thicket of warm brown hair, hazel eyes, and twin dimples that appeared when he smiled…just like his father.

Annie mentally shook the thought out of her head, guilt flooding her when she thought of Derek's black hair and bright green eyes.

What was wrong with her?

She knew coming home and being in her old bedroom would bring back the past whether she wanted to think about it or not. She just hadn't expected the memories to rush in so quickly.

The room seemed to lose its air all of a sudden, Annie's chest feeling tight. Leaving her suitcase half-unpacked on the bed, she stepped back out to the living room. What she really needed was to get out of the house for a few minutes to clear her head.

"Hey, I feel really bad about Dad's dinner," she said, looking at Hannah, who had just finished cleaning up the spilled food. "Is Slice of Paradise still in business?"

"You bet it is," her father replied. "Still the best pizza in a hundred miles, too."

"Great. If it's all right with Hannah, I'm going to go pick up a large pie for all three of us."

Hannah nodded. "Sounds good to me. Want company?"

"No, I can handle it. It's the least I can do after ruining that amazing-looking catfish."

"Okay," Hannah said, flashing her a grateful look. "Call me if you get lost."

Annie laughed, feeling lighter already. "This town is only five square miles. I'm sure I won't get lost."

Hannah smiled. "It's really good to have you back home again, sis."

Emotion pricked the backs of Annie's eyes as she looked at the two people who meant the most to her in the world. The only two people she had left now.

"It feels really good to be home again, too," she said, meaning it from the bottom of her still-broken heart.

CHAPTER 2

"No! You can't be serious," a teenage voice complained.

Another student chimed in, too. "They can't do that!"

Sighing, Noah Davis crossed his arms over his chest and slowly shook his head at the high schoolers in his science club. As a biology teacher, he loved hosting the club for fellow science lovers, but funding had become an issue this year. Or, rather, the lack of funding.

"The town has to make some cuts to fit with the budget. Other school clubs might get cut, too," Noah explained to them as he perched on the edge of his wooden desk, his gaze sweeping over the eleven teenagers in his classroom.

One of the seniors scoffed, slouching at a desk in the back of the room. "We don't even ask for that much money, Mr. Davis."

"We do take more field trips than the other clubs. We were probably targeted because of that," Noah pointed out, preferring to be honest with them. He didn't see his students as kids. He saw them as young adults, and some of them were about to graduate and go off to college. It saddened him to see them leave, but he wanted each of his students to succeed. His job was to help prepare them for that.

"It's probably because we have the best club," a sophomore girl huffed as she crossed her arms, her dark hair falling into her eyes. "Everyone else is just jealous of us."

Noah couldn't help but crack a small smile, despite the seriousness of the situation. It wasn't fair that his club was being singled out, but he had a feeling he knew why he'd been named among the first wave of cuts. It didn't help to have a bitter ex-wife on the school board, who had a hand in deciding what was cut and what was safe.

"This will be our last meeting, unfortunately," Noah told them as he clasped his hands together in front of him. "I hope I'll be able to start the club again when the school has enough funding to keep us active."

When he had been a student here at Crestpoint High, there wasn't a budget problem. He was a tutor and had participated in plenty of clubs without having to worry about any of his extracurricular activities being cut. He just wished he could do more now, because his kids genuinely enjoyed learning about science. He took them to the beach to study some of the creatures that washed up on the shore, and they even found interesting shells and shark's teeth to take for souvenirs. Now, that was all over.

"We can hold the club in secret," another girl suggested, prompting a few intrigued looks from the other students. "We won't tell anyone, Mr. Davis."

Frustrated, Noah lifted his hand up to the back of his neck and into his brown hair. He wished he had good news to give the kids, but all he could offer them was hope for the future.

"As cool as a secret science club sounds, I don't want any

of us getting in trouble with the school or the board." Noah chuckled before glancing toward the clock on the wall behind him. "It's 3:45. You guys should head on home. I promise I'll update you as soon as I hear anything more."

Disappointed sighs and sad goodbyes echoed through the biology classroom as the students gathered their things and walked past empty lab tables and untouched lab equipment to leave. Only one girl remained, a junior with shoulder-length waves the same brown color as his hair. Her shoulders sagged as she remained at her desk.

"Lainey, please don't be upset." Noah sighed as he approached his daughter. He wasn't even sure if she liked science all that much, but she'd insisted that she try his club out. Her disappointment was worse than anyone else's. He felt like he was personally letting his own daughter down now.

"I know Mom cut the club. She's on the board," Lainey muttered, lowering her head so much that her hair fell against her face.

Even though he was at odds with Claudia, Noah still tried to be as respectful as possible when it came to talking about his ex-wife in front of their daughter. He wouldn't stoop that low, no matter how rocky things were between Claudia and him.

"It's not only her decision," Noah replied as he placed a hand on Lainey's shoulder over the stiff fabric of her jean jacket. He gave her a little nudge, trying to lift her spirits.

Lainey tilted her head to gaze up at him with hazel eyes that were more brown than green today. She took after him more than she did her mother in a lot of ways, including his sense of humor and his laidback nature. It didn't make Lainey love her mother any less, but Noah understood it was slightly harder for Lainey to get along with Claudia and her more rigid nature.

"I just know how much you love the club, Dad." Lainey sighed as she moved to stand up, slinging her black backpack onto her shoulder.

His smart, sensitive daughter had a habit of worrying about him. Ever since the divorce happened five years ago, Lainey worried about him being all alone. He didn't want her to spend her childhood stressing about him, despite his own failures and regrets.

Even if marriage hadn't worked out between Claudia and him, he wasn't ready to give up on living yet. He wasn't even ready to give up on love, never mind that his daughter seemed to be afraid he was destined for permanent bachelorhood at the ripe old age of thirty-five.

"I feel like you're more upset about this whole situation than I am," Noah said. He laughed softly, giving her a concerned look. Something more was up that she wasn't telling him. "What's this really about?"

Lainey shrugged, casting her eyes down to her scuffed black Converse sneakers. "I don't know what club to join now. How am I supposed to figure out what I want to do for a career if all of the clubs get cut?"

Noah was lucky to have figured out that he wanted to teach early on during his high school years. It seemed Lainey wasn't having as much luck, but she was still just a junior. He wished she wouldn't worry about her future so much that it made it hard for her to enjoy the years that she had left in school.

"Hey, I promise you'll figure it out, okay?" Noah assured her with a warm smile. "But just know that even your dad at his ancient age still hasn't gotten it all figured out. At sixteen, you're doing just fine."

"Yeah, okay," Lainey sighed with a small nod, her shoulders loosening a degree as she tried to take her father's advice and relax.

"Come on. Let's go grab some pizza, yeah? That always makes you feel better." Noah didn't want her day to be completely ruined. He wouldn't mind some comfort food either, and Slice of Paradise was Crestpoint Beach's staple source of greasy, cheesy goodness.

Lainey finally cracked a smile as she playfully shoulder-bumped her father.

"A large with mushrooms and sausage," she said as they made their way out of the classroom.

Noah slung an arm around her shoulders. "Mushrooms are gross, kid."

"You just have no taste," Lainey quipped with a smirk.

Noah chuckled. He would really miss her once she went off to college. He didn't feel all that lonely when it was his week with Lainey, but the weeks he didn't have her always felt long and empty. He hadn't tried dating all that much since the divorce because he just hadn't felt that connection with anyone yet.

It didn't help that Crestpoint Beach's available female population was small, and consisted primarily of young women who'd graduated high school sometime during his tenure or their divorced moms, both of which were off limits in terms of dating.

It probably also didn't help that when it came to women in general, his ideal partner had some high hurdles to clear. Hurdles that had been set by someone he'd once loved with all his heart, then foolishly let slip away.

At any rate, he was busy enough with his teaching and Lainey. He wasn't looking to start a relationship with anyone new. If he were to meet that special someone, he figured he'd know it when he saw her.

Once he and Lainey walked into the small pizza shop on the corner of Lincoln and Peppertree, Noah ordered them a pizza with mushrooms and sausage on one side, and banana peppers and pepperoni on the other side. He turned away from the ordering counter and walked across the black-and-white tile floor to the wooden table Lainey had reserved for them near the window at the front of the restaurant.

"Shouldn't be too long of a wait. Do you have a lot of homework tonight?" Noah asked once he sat down across from her, dragging his soda cup closer to him so he could sip from the paper straw.

"Just some biology reading," Lainey replied in a pointed tone as she crossed her arms over her chest.

Noah chuckled and shrugged at her. He had made it clear to her early on that in his class, she would receive no special consideration just because they were family. He had to treat her just like all of the other students. However, he could mess with her a little more.

"You need to be familiar with the different ecosystems and the organisms that live there," Noah replied. "It's important stuff."

"What if I never need to know that for my future career?" Lainey asked, lifting her eyebrows at Noah as if she was trying to make a point.

Noah received these questions all the time, especially when he taught his students about cellular structure and other lessons they deemed unimportant to learn unless they intended to become scientists.

"Have you thought about a career in science?" he asked, knowing she had the intelligence and drive to be anything she wanted. "It's getting close to the time that you should be thinking about your major for college. Have you got ideas about anything you'd like to do for a career?"

Lainey wilted a little at the question and shook her head, looking lost all over again.

"Then it's important to learn as many different things as you can so you can figure that out. Obviously, you don't like science the same way I do, so I wouldn't recommend a medical career path." Noah raised a brow, drawing an amused smile to his daughter's face.

"Blood makes me want to vomit," Lainey replied, wrinkling her nose out of disgust.

He chuckled. "You are definitely my kid."

He saw a lot of himself in Lainey, which he suspected was why Claudia was tougher on her than she needed to be, urging Lainey to work hard and figure out her path in life. Claudia mistook common teenage confusion for laziness.

"Order fifty-four! Half mushroom and sausage, half banana peppers and pepperoni!" Stan Romano, the old man working the counter, barked into a microphone, his voice echoing throughout the whole pizza shop.

"That's us. I'll be right back." Noah stood, then began winding his way through the maze of tables to get to the counter. He saw a flash of sleek blonde hair out of the corner of his eye, making him pause to let the slender woman beside him move to the front. "You can go ahead."

"Oh, no, it's okay. You were here first," she replied as she reached up to tuck a loose strand of straight blonde hair behind her ear, better revealing her pretty face and unforgettable blue eyes.

It felt like Noah had been struck by a train. He never expected to see her around here again after she had left all those years ago. Seventeen years, his heart reminded him with a heavy thump. Yet she was somehow right there in front of him again.

"Annie?" He managed to breathe out in shock, his eyes widening as if he had seen a ghost.

She tilted her head up to him, looking about as shocked as he felt. "Noah."

"What are you doing here?" he asked, frowning in confusion. It took him a second to realize how unfriendly he must seem. "Sorry, that didn't come out right. What I mean is, I thought you were in Dallas."

She gave him a weak smile. "I was. I came home to spend some time with Dad and Hannah. I drove in today, actually. I'm sure I must look like I just drove eleven hours straight, too."

He shook his head. She looked amazing to him, still girl-next-door beautiful in her faded, loose-fitting jeans, T-shirt, and flats. She'd always been tall and lean, from grade school through senior high.

Now that he was really looking at her, she seemed a little thinner than he recalled, and he was guessing the shadows under her clear blue eyes probably had as much to do with grief as they did the long drive home to Crestpoint Beach.

"Frank told me about your husband's accident. I'm sorry for your loss, Annie."

"Thank you." She glanced down for a moment before meeting his gaze again, a questioning look in her eyes. "I didn't realize you kept in touch with my dad."

Noah shrugged, not wanting her to think he'd been prying into her personal life, even if he did ask about her with Frank

Taylor more often than he probably had a right to. "It's a small town. He and I run into each other now and then." Noah cleared his throat. "How's he doing?"

"He's good. His arthritis is getting to be a problem, though. That's actually why I came back. I wanted to help Hannah look after him for a while."

Noah smiled. "I know they'll both appreciate having you home."

He found it hard to believe she'd been away seventeen years, minus the handful of times he'd heard she was in town visiting her family. He had made it a point to be scarce around town during those times, hoping to avoid any awkward run-ins after the way he'd left things with Annie the night of their senior prom.

This unexpected face-to-face meeting felt anything but awkward. It had always been easy to talk with her, just one of the reasons she'd stolen his heart in third grade when they were best friends, and kept it all the way through high school. Longer than that, if he was being honest with himself. It had taken him years to get over her, if he ever truly had.

As for the way he'd hurt her and drove her away from the hometown, he didn't think he'd ever forgive himself for that. His only consolation was the fact that she'd gone on to make a great life and career for herself in Dallas…at least, until it all fell apart.

He hated that she'd endured even more hurt after leaving their hometown. Now that she was back, maybe he would have the chance to make amends for his part, at least.

"How long are you planning to be in town?"

"I'm not sure yet," she said, folding her arms in front of her. "I don't have a job now, so I'll have to find work before too long."

Noah nodded. "There's a great home furnishings store downtown now, Seaside Designs. They do a lot of work for the new houses going up along the beachfront. Maybe they can hook you up with some interior design clients."

"Thanks for the tip." Annie tilted her head at him. "What about you? Are you still doing crazy lab experiments in your mom's garage, and shooting off homemade rockets over at the park?"

He chuckled. "More or less, I guess you could say. I teach high school biology now."

"Really?" She laughed. "That's great, Noah. And so you."

Her smile still had the power to light up the entire room. Or, in this case, the entire pizza parlor. As they talked, other customers brushed past them to place or pick up orders. Noah hardly noticed the jostle and noise. His full attention was on Annie.

Against his will, his mind flashed back to a spring day in fifth grade—the day he worked up the courage to kiss Annie Taylor at recess. It had been an innocent peck on the lips under a huge, old oak tree at the far end of the elementary school playground, but that kiss haunted him to this day. It had been the day he realized he loved Annie, and that she loved him too.

A lot of time had passed since then, but standing with her now brought it all back in vivid color. In spite of how he'd messed things up with her as a cowardly high school senior, being with her now felt as natural as breathing.

He noticed her gaze moving past him now and then, toward the other side of the restaurant dining room. He glanced behind him and saw Lainey peering his way in obvious curiosity.

Annie gave him a quizzical look. "One of your admiring students, Mr. Davis?"

He grinned. "Ah, that's my daughter, Lainey. She's not known for her subtlety, especially where I'm concerned."

"You have a daughter?" Annie's smile seemed to falter a little. "I didn't know you were married."

"I was," he said. "I've been divorced for five years now."

"Oh. I'm sorry. I hope it wasn't difficult for you or Lainey."

"Well, I wouldn't say it's been easy, but we're doing our best."

A raspy bellow boomed over the dining room loudspeaker. "Order fifty-four! You gonna pick up, or what?"

Annie giggled. "I see Old Man Romano is as customer-friendly as always."

Noah chuckled. "Some things never change."

"You'd better grab that pie before he starts auctioning it off."

"Yeah." His feet seemed rooted to the floor. His gaze was unwilling to leave hers, too. "I guess I'll see you around, Annie."

She gave him a polite nod. "See you, Noah."

Reluctantly, he moved ahead of her to fetch his pizza. As he brought the box over to a wide-eyed Lainey, he couldn't help glancing back to where Annie now stood placing her order at the counter.

"Dad, who is that?" Lainey asked, ignoring the food to gape at him in avid interest.

"Her name's Annie. She's a girl I used to know."

"She's really pretty."

"Yes, she is."

"So?" Lainey prompted. "Are you just gonna sit here, or are you gonna ask her out?"

He snapped out of his distraction with Annie to frown at his daughter. "I'm not asking anyone out. Eat your pizza before it gets cold."

"Fine."

While Lainey attacked the sausage-and-mushroom side, Noah watched Annie step away from the counter to sit at an empty table to wait for her order. She seemed determined to avoid looking at him now, busying herself with her phone and keeping her head down.

If she didn't want to invite more conversation with him, it was probably for the best. Maybe she had only been being polite, making small talk because she felt obligated to be friendly with someone she used to know. After all, she had only been widowed for nine months. What kind of man would be staring at her and wondering if she might still have even a fraction of the feelings Noah still harbored for her?

It took surprising effort to tear his gaze away from her again, but somehow he managed.

"How's all that gross fungus on your pizza, kiddo?"

Lainey grinned around a big mouthful. "Delicious."

With a chuckle, Noah pulled out a piece from his side of the pie and started eating.

CHAPTER 3

It was taking Annie a little longer than she anticipated it would to get her bearings in Crestpoint Beach. As familiar as everything seemed, nothing was the same now.

Her father had retired from his job as lighthouse keeper years ago. Free-spirited Hannah had forgone college and was working at the local gift shop. Annie was glad to see her talented sister embracing her artistic side, too. In her spare time, Hannah made seashell crafts and other quirky home decorations.

And then there was Noah.

It had been three days since she ran into him at Slice of Paradise, but he hadn't been far from her thoughts in the time since. She wasn't surprised he'd gone into teaching. He'd always had a love for exploring and learning new things. His calm, confident manner and easy sense of humor probably made him a favorite with his students. Annie was sure all of Noah's positive qualities also made him a great father to Lainey.

She felt bad about his divorce, especially considering how hard Noah had taken his own parents' breakup when he was in grade school. Annie had done her best to help him through the trauma of his father walking out on him and his mom, just like Noah had been there for her when her mom lost her battle with cancer.

They had been best friends in those days. She had foolishly believed they would be best friends, and more, for the rest of their lives.

"Come on, Annie!" Hannah's voice sounded from the living room, echoing all the way into Annie's bedroom. A moment later, she stood in the open doorway, a broad smile on her face. "What are you doing in here? It's too gorgeous of a day to spend it cooped up inside. Let's go have some fun."

"What kind of fun?"

"You'll see. Come on!"

Narrowing her eyes in confusion, Annie moved off the bed and followed Hannah through the little house. Their father glanced up and offered her a warm smile.

"Do you know what this is about, Dad?"

"Just go and see," he encouraged her with a nod.

Annie sighed, a small smile crossing her lips. "All right. Lead the way, Hannah."

It meant a lot to her that her father and sister were doing everything in their power to try to make her feel welcome over the past few days that she had been home. They were practically on top of one another in the small bungalow now that she was there, too, but neither of them seemed to mind. At times, Annie longed for her privacy, especially when her grief over Derek crept up on her at unexpected moments. But she also enjoyed being around her family, whether they were all cleaning the kitchen together after a meal or watching their favorite sitcom together in the living room.

Hannah led Annie to the beach a few streets away from the bungalow. When they reached the sand and Hannah headed right with purpose, Annie realized where they were going. Still, she couldn't keep the wonder out of her voice once they stopped in front of the sky-blue Victorian with its white gingerbread trim and wide, wraparound porch.

"Grandma and Grandpa's beach house."

Hannah smiled. "I thought you'd like to see it."

Annie nodded, taking it all in. The house held so many memories. She and her family had lived there with her maternal grandparents from the time Annie was born until a few months after her mom had passed when Annie was eight and Hannah was three. Grandpa Joe was already gone by then, and not long after the funeral for Annie's mom, Grandma Betsy suffered a stroke and had to be moved into a nursing home for the handful of months she'd had left. Annie's dad then decided to downsize from the six-bedroom, five-bath Victorian to the smaller bungalow, where he'd continued to raise his girls on his own.

But before all of that sadness, the beach house had been full of happy times. Annie couldn't count all the days she'd spent making sandcastles with Hannah and their mom on the beach just steps away from the veranda, or swaying back and forth on the porch swing with Grandma Betsy while they sipped lemonade and watched the dolphins play in the waves.

The big flower beds that ran around the perimeter of the house were overgrown now and in need of regular tending, but some of the pink chrysanthemums and beach roses were still peeking out of the weeds.

Annie looked at her sister. "Weren't you living here at one time?"

"I was for a few years, but Dad was starting to get worse. He needed me more at home, so I moved back in with him." Hannah led Annie up to the front door, pulling a silver key out of her pocket to unlock it. "Want to go inside?"

"Yes!"

Once the door drifted open, Annie peered inside, stepping over the threshold to observe a bare, dusty space. With only a few shrouded pieces of furniture left inside, the layout of the beach house was open and airy, with large, shuttered windows overlooking the beach and green-blue waves.

Five of the bedrooms spread out between the first and second floor, with a large apartment space and dedicated bathroom encompassing the third floor. The kitchen had older appliances, but Grandma Betsy had been a meticulous housekeeper, so everything still looked to be in decent shape. Something would need to be done about all of the dust and cobwebs, though.

"It's still as beautiful as I remember it," Annie said, taking a brief walk around.

"Yep, it is," Hannah agreed. "It'll be even more beautiful once you spruce it up."

"Me?"

Hannah nodded. "Dad and I talked about this. We want you to have it."

"Have it?" Annie practically stuttered. "The whole house?"

"It only seems right to keep it in the family, don't you agree?"

She didn't know what to say. She hadn't expected anything like this to happen when Hannah dragged her out of the house. She thought they were going shopping, or grabbing some breakfast muffins from Dockside Donuts.

"This house is huge, Hannah. It's much too big for just me. Besides, what about you?"

"I'm happy back at the house with Dad. I know you like designing and stuff, so I figured you could fix up the beach house for yourself or for anything that you wanted. It's a lot of space to work with, but I'm sure you'll think of something." A hopeful look crossed Hannah's face as she smiled at Annie. "Maybe Dad and I are hoping the house will give you a reason to stay in Crestpoint Beach. As in, for good."

"Hannah," Annie said, reaching out to draw her sister in for a hug. "You and Dad are plenty of reason for me to stay. I just need to figure out what I'm going to do for work, and that might mean I'll have to take a job in a bigger city nearby."

"Or maybe you'll find work here," Hannah suggested, a bright smile on her face as she stepped out of Annie's embrace. "You could use the beach house to showcase your interior design work. You could even fix it up and open it as a bed and breakfast!"

Annie laughed. "I haven't even said yes to taking the house yet."

"Then say yes. Dad and I really do want you to have it."

Annie was speechless for a few moments as she took in the news. The beach house was actually hers if she wanted it. Her imagination raced ahead to all the ways she could improve the place and bring it back to its former glory. It wouldn't take much. A deep cleaning and some fresh paint inside and out, a few repairs and updates, new furnishings and window treatments. All the house needed was some time and attention, along with a little elbow grease and determination—all things she had in abundance at the moment.

She had to admit, it was the perfect project for her to focus on. Ever since Derek died, she hadn't worked on anything design-wise. In addition to her sorrow and the very real concerns about their shared business and a home they really couldn't afford, she simply hadn't been inspired to take on something new. Now, she could hardly wait to flesh out her ideas for the beach house.

Annie breathed out, excitement fluttering in her chest in almost the same way it had a few days ago when she saw Noah Davis in person for the first time in seventeen years. "All right, I'll say yes to fixing up the house. On one condition."

"Name it."

"I want you to help me."

"Me? Really?" Hannah asked, a shocked look coming onto her face.

Annie nodded. "I could use your artistic flair. I'm sure you have lots of great ideas that would add some extra color and life to this place."

Despite both of them having a love for art and style, Hannah had a playful sense of whimsy and creativity, while Annie was more reserved and classic in her choices. Together, they would make a well-balanced team.

Besides that, Annie knew Hannah had felt some pressure being the younger of them. Annie's ambition and serious-minded career goals had cast a bit of a heavy shadow on Hannah. However, Hannah seemed as happy working the gift shop and making her art in the hometown as Annie had been when she landed her big studio job in Dallas.

As sisters, they had been close growing up, but Annie knew she could've come up with more ways for them to bond, especially before she fled the state for so many years. She had left everyone behind. For as long as she could remain in Crestpoint Beach, Annie hoped she could repair the strong bond she used to have with both her father and Hannah.

Hannah placed her hands on her hips, a thoughtful look crossing her face as her gaze panned the room. "We should paint each wall a different color of the rainbow!"

A laugh burst from Annie. It really was nice being back home.

She shook her head, draping her arm over Hannah's shoulders to draw her closer. "Tell you what. Let's make a plan, then we'll decide on major changes. Including any potential rainbow color schemes."

"Oh, fine." Hannah giggled as she clung to Annie's side in a warm embrace. She motioned for Annie to follow her out to the stairs leading down from the veranda, moving to sit on the bottom step. She kicked her sneakers off and stuck her feet in the sand, sighing contently as she looked out toward the ocean.

Annie sat beside her and followed suit as she listened to the rush of the waves. The beach always had the power to sweep away all of Annie's worries and doubts, at least for a little while. The idea of living this close to the water again felt like a little piece of heaven.

"How does it feel being back home again?" Hannah asked after they'd sat together in comfortable silence for a few minutes.

"It feels…good," Annie admitted. "Different, but good. It kind of feels like I'm stepping back in time. So much is familiar and comfortable, yet nothing is quite the same as when I left."

Hannah nodded, studying her. "You've been gone a long time. Life keeps moving forward. People do, too."

Noah immediately came to Annie's mind. It had been a shock seeing him again. Admittedly, he looked good, even better than he had in high school. Now, the lanky teen was a tall, athletically built man whose lean face had matured into handsome angles and a strong, squared jaw. He still had the thick brown hair that used to feel so soft against her fingertips, and his hazel eyes now gleamed with as much seasoned confidence as they did easy humor.

His daughter was beautiful, too. Why the thought of Noah having been married and a father should put a knot of regret inside her, Annie didn't want to know.

Still, she couldn't help but wonder about all of the life she had missed out on by running away from Crestpoint Beach to pursue her education and career. If she had stayed...

If she had stayed, she would have walked away from a full-ride scholarship at University of Texas. She never would have had her amazing career with one of Dallas's top interior design firms, and she never would have met Derek, either. Annie wouldn't want to trade any of those things, even now.

As a senior at Crestpoint High, madly in love with Noah Davis, she wouldn't have known what was waiting for her somewhere else.

"I ran into Noah the other day," she confided quietly. There was no reason to use his last name with Hannah, or to remind her sister of what he'd been to Annie. Everyone in town knew she and Noah had been inseparable all through school. Annie's family was no exception.

"You ran into him...when?"

"The other afternoon at Slice of Paradise."

Hannah gaped at her. "The day you got here? And you didn't tell me?"

Annie shrugged, smiling. "I'm telling you now."

"So, did you talk to him?"

"A little bit. He mentioned he's teaching at the high school now. I was glad to hear that. He was always great at tutoring. I wouldn't have passed half my exams without his helping me to study for them."

Annie remembered their many study dates in the library or at each other's houses. Noah was patient and kind with her, always talking out each problem until she understood it fully. It was part of the reason she was so confused when he randomly stopped talking to her in the days leading up to prom. Right before he humiliated her and broke her heart by standing her up the night of the dance.

Her anger had faded long ago, the confusion lingered even now. Along with the hurt.

"The kids love him," Hannah said. She leaned over, nudging Annie with her shoulder. "I know you did too,"

Annie didn't deny it. How could she? He had been her first kiss, her first date, her first love. They had more good times and silly adventures together than she could count. He'd also helped her through tough tests, heavy emotions, and daunting obstacles. She wouldn't have made it to graduation without him, even if the last few months of her senior year were some of the worst of her life after they broke up.

"Noah's daughter was with him at the pizza place."

"Lainey," Hannah confirmed. "She's a good kid, smart like her dad…and her mom. Did Noah tell you he's divorced now?"

Annie tried to ignore the sing-song way her sister presented that newsflash. "Yes, he mentioned it. I feel bad that he went through that."

"I think everyone in town was more shocked when he got married about a year after you left for college."

"Wow, that soon?"

Living in a small town meant knowing everyone else's business, and acknowledging that you were eventually going to be part of the conversation, too. Annie didn't know anything about anyone back in Dallas because there were far too many people all around her. She'd had neighbors for years whom she'd never even met, let alone knew the comings and goings of their personal lives.

Hannah gave her a sympathetic look. "I'm not sure it was totally Noah's idea to get married so soon. I mean, Claudia Harrow went after him like extra credit on a midterm exam the minute you were gone."

Annie nearly groaned at the mention of her class's valedictorian. She and Claudia weren't friends, if Claudia even knew who she was. Smart, popular, and pretty, Claudia had also had a mean streak that probably came part and parcel with her good looks and easy A's. To top it off, she'd even been voted prom queen. Annie could only imagine how high she had risen beyond her high school years. No wonder Noah had fallen for her so quickly after he'd put Annie out of his mind.

"Anyway," Hannah said, "it's been about five years since they divorced. It was kind of rough, from what I've heard, but I think they're both happier on their own. Claudia is on the school board and she also owns one of the boutiques in town."

"Well, I hope for Lainey's sake that Noah and Claudia are in a better place now," Annie said, wondering why they got divorced. Even if Noah wasn't hers to worry about anymore, she couldn't help but be mildly curious about him.

"Things aren't totally rosy," Hannah said, digging up a small coquina shell with one of her multi-colored, painted toenails. "I hear Claudia and the school board have been making cuts to some programs and events around town, including Noah's after-school science club."

Annie frowned, wondering how bad things were for the town. Crestpoint Beach never had financial problems before, and she hated to think they might be struggling to fund important things for area kids.

"I'm sorry to hear that," she murmured, her thoughts drifting to the large life insurance check tucked away in the nightstand back at the bungalow.

The money could be put to good use with a lot of things, once she was ready to let it go. She wasn't there yet, though. Just thinking about spending money she'd received because Derek had died put a cold lump in her throat.

"Hey, I've got a thought," Hannah blurted. "We should go shop around for some ideas for the beach house. I know just the place too. It's called Seaside Designs. You'll love it."

Annie smiled to herself, recognizing the name of the home furnishings store Noah had mentioned to her. Hannah jumped to her feet and slipped her shoes on, motioning for Annie to follow her.

"Come on," Hannah said. "It's close enough that we can walk there."

They headed off the beach and back up to Main Street for a couple of blocks to the attractive, surprisingly large store. A variety of furniture was on display in a couple dozen staged room mock-ups, with lamps of all styles in a lighting area, framed art on the walls, and countless other small décor pieces arranged around the entire store. The space was open and modern, and Annie's designer brain was on happy overload the moment they stepped inside the air-conditioned showroom.

"Hi, welcome to Seaside Design. I'm Zoe. Can I help you guys find anything?"

A young woman approached from a nearby display, greeting them with a cheery smile. As she weaved through the furniture, her curly dark-brown hair bounced around her shoulders. She was pretty, with smooth, mocha-hued skin and beautiful brown eyes.

"Hi, I'm Hannah, and this is my sister, Annie. We're planning to fix up an old beach house, and we're looking for some ideas."

"Nice! Do you have any thoughts about what you like, or are you starting from scratch?" Zoe asked as she adjusted her bright blue apron over a gray button-down shirt and black jeans. A pair of gloves were tucked in her apron, which had a few wood shavings embedded in its fabric.

"We're only just getting started, but I'm thinking along the lines of a coastal calm vibe with room to add some pops of color and whimsy," Annie mused out loud as she gazed around the store, seeing a section in the back that looked promising.

"Perfect. Let me show you some options."

Zoe motioned for them to follow her toward the very section that had caught Annie's eye. Along the way, they passed one beautiful room design after another, and white shelves lined with different accent pieces ranging from vases to curtains to patio string lights.

Annie could see why Noah had recommended the store as a potential resource for her if she decided to pursue design work in town. The place was packed with everything from budget room outfits to high-end items she recognized from her client work in Dallas.

"Have you worked here very long?" Hannah asked Zoe.

"Usually, I see Mrs. Keller's son working the floor when I pass by on my way to my shift at the gift shop."

Zoe glanced over at Hannah with a surprised look, like she didn't expect anyone to notice she was new. "Gordie's home with a cold, so I'm filling in. Usually, I'm in back working on repairs and refurbs. I moved here from Las Vegas a few months ago."

Hannah nodded. "Cool. I've always wanted to visit Vegas. Annie just moved home from Texas," she added, flashing a smile at Annie and encouraging her to jump into the conversation.

"The city is a lot different from Crestpoint Beach," Annie added, trying to overcome her awkwardness. It wasn't as if she didn't have friends, but she had become something of a hermit after Derek passed. It was strange being social again, acting as though everything in her life was going back to normal.

"I'm still getting used to the difference," Zoe said. "It's eerily quiet here, and I'm never late when I have to drive somewhere because there's hardly any traffic." Zoe laughed softly as she grabbed a few furniture catalogs off one of the shelves.

Annie smiled. "It's almost too quiet here. If it wasn't for the rumble of the waves at night, I don't think I'd be able to sleep at all."

"Same, girl," Zoe agreed.

"Wait, if it's too quiet, neither one of you can fall asleep?" Hannah asked them, pitching them a confused look.

"When you're around noise so long, you get used to hearing it. When you don't hear it anymore, it almost unnerves you," Zoe explained as she set the thick product catalogs down on a nearby table and opened them to pages she seemed to know instinctively would be in line with Annie's tastes. And she wasn't wrong, either.

Hannah sighed wistfully. "I don't think I could ever leave the sound of the ocean. There's nothing more relaxing."

Zoe gave her a lighthearted shrug. "I do like the sound of waves more than cars honking in the middle of the night. Annie, what do you think of these looks?"

She glanced at the overstuffed, yet classic, living room furnishings that looked so comfortable and inviting she wished she had them in the beach house already. "This is exactly the kind of vibe I was imagining, Zoe. What do you think, Hannah?"

Her sister smiled, nodding eagerly. "Perfect."

Zoe laughed softly. "I love those room ideas, too."

"Is it all right if we take some photos for reference?" Annie asked. "We're going to need to start a binder of all our plans and ideas."

"Of course." Zoe returned to the samples display, retrieving a couple more catalogs for them to browse. "I grew up in a big city. I always thought that was the life was for me, but…things change. I prefer the peace I've found here. I guess maybe I just needed a soft place to land. Plus, the people are pretty nice so far."

Annie and Hannah exchanged a smile.

Zoe put the new books down in front of them. "So, Hannah, you said you work at the gift shop. What about you, Annie?"

"Oh, I'm…in between things right now. Just trying to figure out the rest of my life."

"Who isn't, right?"

"Annie's a brilliant interior designer," Hannah interjected. At Annie's flat look, she giggled. "Well, it's true."

Zoe tilted her head. "You should talk to Mrs. Keller, the store owner. I'll bet she'd be willing to post your info on the website, or even recommend you to customers who need a designer. I can put a word in for you."

Annie sighed, touched by her sweet offer. She had forgotten how it felt to be part of a small community, even her own hometown. In Dallas, everyone was viewed as competition. There were only so many prime positions, space, and opportunities to go around. Here, everyone looked out for each other regardless of the opportunity, and Zoe was no exception, even though she was a relative newcomer to Crestpoint Beach. Annie had a feeling she and Hannah had found an instant friend today.

"Thank you for offering to help me out. Maybe when I'm ready to get back to work, I'll stop by and introduce myself to Mrs. Keller."

"Great," Zoe said, her gaze lingering as if she could tell Annie was dealing with more than just a change in jobs or locations. "I'll be here if you need me."

While they talked, Hannah drifted over to a collection of vanities. Naturally, the one that caught her eye was a cute, quirky piece made of polished wood that had a wave-like design carved into the legs.

"How adorable is this, Annie?"

She nodded, having to admit the whimsical, ocean-inspired piece made her smile, too. "I love it. What do you think, should we get it?"

Even though the beach house renovation was supposed to be her project, she liked input from others and she truly wanted Hannah to contribute her own ideas as well. Annie knew it always helped to draw influence from others to get the best output. She had been on her own long enough to learn that lesson in various circumstances.

Besides, it did her heart good to see her sister light up with excitement as she was doing now.

"Are you serious?"

Annie nodded. The vanity was obviously handcrafted by someone who'd taken a lot of care and put a great deal of attention into it. The price reflected that effort, but if they had been shopping in Dallas, they would have to pay twice as much or more.

Zoe cleared her throat. "I actually made that piece."

"You did?" Hannah beamed. "It's amazing."

Zoe blushed, a proud smile on her lips. "Thanks. Making furniture is a hobby of mine."

"It should be more than a hobby," Annie murmured, imagining the piece in front of one of the bedroom windows that faced the water. What better way get ready for the day than by facing the ocean while doing it?

"How about a dining table for guests?" Hannah asked. "We can't have them eating off the floor."

Annie was about to ask what guests they would be expecting, but she stopped herself. Hannah was having too much fun dreaming, and maybe Annie wanted to take a page out of her sister's book and hope for a brighter future.

"Zoe, could you show us what you have for dining room options?" Annie asked with a warm smile, realizing that this project would heal in more ways than one. She just had to open herself up to that change, but that was easier said than done.

CHAPTER 4

Frustrated shouts and angry words filled the empty parking lot in front of Crestpoint High, growing louder as the argument with Claudia escalated.

Most of the students and staff had left for the day, but since it was Claudia's week with Lainey, she'd come to pick up their daughter after her Geometry make-up test that afternoon. It hadn't taken long for Claudia to find something to argue about with Noah.

"I am not a bad father, and she is not a lazy kid. You have no right to assume that of your own daughter." It was generally pointless to argue with her, but he would always defend Lainey.

Claudia flipped her auburn hair over her shoulder and narrowed a glare at him. "You let her skip school to go on a trip with a friend. How is that responsible in any way, Noah? As a teacher and as her father, you should be encouraging her to follow the rules, not break them. She needs to be focused on school."

"It was an excursion to Turtle Island for a few hours. It

was as much of an opportunity to study as it was to have a little fun. The kids are learning about the island's plants and marine life in my class." Noah knew Claudia wouldn't care for any of his explanations. He could go around and around with her, but nothing would change. Her unwillingness to negotiate was one of the reasons for their divorce, among others.

"Well, I don't like it," she huffed, crossing her arms over her sultry figure, which was donned in an emerald-green wrap dress straight out of her boutique, Harrow's Cove. "Lainey needs structure and discipline, not vacations. You're lucky her grades aren't slipping yet. Then, there would be real consequences for both of you."

Noah wanted to throw his hands up, but he merely folded his arms over his white button-down shirt and black blazer, determined to keep his cool. Claudia could come after the quality of his parenting all she wanted, but Lainey didn't deserve to be dragged into the fight when she had done nothing wrong.

"She's doing perfectly fine, Claudia. She gets A's in all of her classes, and despite what you seem to think, she's a hardworking, responsible kid. She didn't like that you cut my science club, though, and I have to say that I didn't appreciate it either."

Claudia rolled her eyes, glancing toward the front of the building briefly before looking back at him. "Your club costs the school too much money for your supplies and field trips. It was a necessary cut."

"How much more are you and the board going to cut? Aside from disappointing a lot of kids, I've also been hearing from other teachers and parents who aren't happy about what you've already gotten rid of," Noah pointed out, wondering how extensive the damage would be. His colleagues were starting to get nervous, hoping their organizations or events weren't next to be axed.

Claudia sighed as she leaned against her white Mercedes SUV. "The annual budget is already stretched thin in crucial areas. Spending has been out of control for several years before I joined the board, so now it's time to tighten our belts. We're doing damage control at this point to keep things from getting any worse." She pursed her lips as she stared at him, as if she had more to say. "There's a town meeting on Saturday that you should come to. We'll be announcing other cuts then."

"Yeah, I'll be there." Noah exhaled heavily as he swept his hand through his hair. He hoped things would turn around soon. Crestpoint Beach wouldn't be the same without all of its community events and organizations.

The doors to the front of the school suddenly opened, as Lainey and a red-headed boy wearing a Pink Floyd T-shirt walked outside. Lainey smiled shyly at the boy before waving goodbye and heading over to her parents, a light blush filling her cheeks.

Noah recognized the boy as Mason Simmons, an inspiring musician and songwriter who had recently formed a band with some of his friends. He was a good kid, one Noah didn't mind hanging around his daughter. Before he could greet Lainey, Claudia stepped forward.

"Isn't that the Simmons boy? I thought I told you no dating in high school?"

Lainey's shoulders drooped, her bright glow dimming as her mother chastised her even before she greeted her. "I'm not dating him. Mason was just being nice and walking me out," she murmured, lowering her eyes to the ground.

Claudia continued her rant. "What is he still doing here at

the school so late? Was he in detention? You don't need to be hanging out with people like that, Lainey."

Noah broke into the conversation, unwilling to stand by and let Claudia bully their daughter. She hadn't done anything wrong. "Calm down, Claudia. He's a band kid. They have practice after school."

"Don't tell me to calm down," she snapped. "Someone has to keep an eye on our daughter, and it obviously won't be you." She moved to get into the vehicle, gesturing for Lainey to follow her. "Tell your father goodbye."

Lainey turned to Noah with a soft sigh, flashing him a quick, grateful look before embracing him. "I'm sorry about this."

"Don't worry about me," Noah told her quietly, placing his hand on the back of her head to hold her close. "How was your test?"

"Piece of cake," Lainey replied, pulling away and smiling at him. "I'll see you around school, Dad. I love you."

"Love you too, kid."

Noah walked with her to the passenger side of the SUV and opened the door for her, then waited for her to get situated before he closed her inside with her mother. He looked over at Claudia, receiving a cold look before she sped away from the school.

Noah sighed as he watched the Mercedes disappear down the street, a heavy feeling in his chest. He couldn't believe he had spent so much of his life married to the wrong woman. The only good thing that had come from them being together was Lainey. Their daughter was worth any amount of stress or poor judgment. He'd made a lot of mistakes since his high school years, but he couldn't regret the one that brought him Lainey.

As for the other colossal mistake he'd made in his youth, he had hardly gone a day without wondering how things might have been different if he hadn't been such a coward with Annie. How often had he wished he could do it over? How often in that first year she was gone away to college in Texas had he been tempted to get in his car and go after her? How often had he started to dial her number to apologize, only to hang up before the call connected?

Now, she was home again.

The timing couldn't be worse, though. She was grieving the loss of her husband and trying to care for her father, while Noah was dealing with a spiteful ex-wife and a teenager who needed her dad more than ever. Never mind his potentially imploding career, if Claudia had her way with the board's budget decisions.

Noah turned and walked back into the school, venturing through the halls until he came across the algebra classroom, where his best friend, Henry Park, was still grading tests. Noah knocked on the door frame before entering and taking a seat on the edge of one of the desks in the front row.

Henry's black brows rose over his almond-shaped eyes as he set down his red pen. "Uh, oh. I know that face. What's wrong?"

A few years younger than Noah, Henry was high energy in everything he did. He often went surfing and boating in his spare time, hardly remaining still, even when he was teaching. His bright smile and youthful attitude in the classroom made him one of the favorites around school.

"It's Claudia's week with Lainey. I just sent her off," Noah muttered, tapping his dark brown dress shoe on the tile flooring. Aside from the unpleasantness of arguing with his ex, he was already missing his daughter and she'd barely been gone ten minutes. Noah never liked the days he didn't have Lainey with him. The reality of how lonely he was really set in, and it was nearly impossible to ignore.

"I'm guessing Claudia gave you grief over something," Henry said as he leaned back in his black spinning chair, propping his black loafers up on the corner of his wooden desk, which was littered with papers and pens.

Noah nodded. "She didn't appreciate me letting Lainey go on that island excursion. It was only for three hours. Claudia acted like I let Lainey skip to go to Disney World or something."

Noah sighed, relieved that he could let his guard down with his friend. They had immediately gravitated toward each other on Henry's first day teaching, bonding over their dislike of the rubbery nature of the school cafeteria's lasagna and their appreciation of the summer break. It didn't take them long to become close friends who felt comfortable commiserating over things happening in their personal lives.

"Obviously, Claudia doesn't like the fact that you let Lainey have more fun than she does. You're the cool parent," Henry pointed out with a small shrug.

"I let Lainey take a break to have fun and relax every once in a while because she's just a kid. She doesn't need to be stressing every second. She'll get plenty of that in adulthood," Noah muttered with a wry smile.

"Tell me about it," Henry chuckled, shaking his head.

"This wasn't where I expected to be at my age," Noah admitted. "Divorced and single again. Trying not to mess up my kid because of it."

He thought he would be settled down and stable at this point in his life. It's all he wanted after learning Claudia was pregnant. He wanted to be the father he didn't have. He had tried to be happy with Claudia. For a while, he'd convinced himself that he was. Eventually, reality set in. It became obvious they couldn't balance out all of their differences. Not even Lainey's birth had saved them.

"You're a great father to Lainey," Henry said. "Don't listen to Claudia. She's clearly got things to work out, but you're not the problem."

Noah smiled. "Thanks for saying that."

"It's the truth. As for being single, don't ask me for advice. I'm still trying to figure that out for myself."

Noah had dreaded the idea of dating from the day he and Claudia split up. He still believed in love, but getting there had never seemed farther away. There was a part of him that felt he'd lost that chance when he broke Annie's heart.

He cleared his throat and glanced at Henry. "You know that girl that I told you I dated in high school, Annie Taylor?"

"Ah, yes. The one that got away." Henry sighed dramatically. "Or should I say, the one you let get away?"

"She's back in town."

Henry shot up straight in his chair, his feet colliding against the floor as he stared at Noah in shock. "She's back? For a visit or for good?"

"I'm not sure how long she'll be here. Her husband passed away nine months ago. She moved back home to be with her family for a while," Noah explained, unable to imagine the pain she must be feeling. Beyond his own selfish reasons for being glad she came home, he knew she had a good family who would give her all the support she needed.

"Wow, that's rough. She's young to be a widow," Henry said as he stood up to walk around to the front of his desk so that he could perch on it. "Have you seen her yet?"

Noah nodded, a small smile pulling at his lips as he

thought back to when he had come across her. "We ran into each other at Slice of Paradise. I thought it would be awkward seeing her again, but it wasn't. And she looks beautiful. Annie always was the prettiest girl in school, but now…"

"Sounds like you still aren't over her all these years later," Henry commented, an intrigued look crossing his face. "I didn't know a crush could last that long,"

"It's not just a crush with her. I really loved Annie."

A part of him always would. He couldn't help but wonder what would've happened if he had been selfish enough to encourage her to stay in Crestpoint Beach instead of going off and chasing her dreams. Would they have been happy? Would she have grown to resent him for holding her back from the education and career she had dreamed of? It was a risk he hadn't been willing to take at the time. He only wished he'd been mature enough to handle the situation differently than he had.

"Why don't you ask her out?" Henry suggested. "You know, nothing serious, just coffee or lunch. You can see if the chemistry is still there, and maybe you guys can try again."

"Did you miss the part where I said her husband just died?"

Henry lowered his chin to regard Noah with a challenging look. "It's been nine months, you said. What can it hurt to invite her out as an old friend? She might enjoy your company."

As tempted as he was, Noah frowned. "What if things are too different between us now? She could be a different person. Maybe I'm different than she remembers, too."

"Well, you won't find out until you sit down and talk to her. I'm sure you owe her an apology for ruining her senior prom anyway," Henry reminded him, amusement in his voice.

Noah glared at Henry, who put his hands up defensively. Noah knew he had no room to balk at what Henry said, because he was right. He had ruined Annie's prom, but that was better than possibly ruining her life.

As if Henry sensed his indecision, he reached out and cuffed Noah's shoulder. "You're a good guy. You'll know when the time is right. Just get to know her all over again, okay? We don't get many second chances in life."

Noah knew Henry had a point. Yes, things were different now, for both Annie and him. They needed to get to know each other as friends again, especially if she decided to stay.

And if she decided not to stay?

He didn't want to consider that option. Now that she was back, it was going to be even harder to see her leave again.

Henry was right about second chances. They were rare.

About as rare as a woman like Annie.

He slanted a wry look at Henry. "Aren't you the guy who just told me not to come looking for dating advice from you?"

Henry grinned. "That was me from five minutes ago, and before you mentioned you'd run into your Annie."

His Annie.

That was how he'd always thought about her growing up. His best friend. His first love. His one and only.

Was there anything left of what they used to have together?

Noah supposed there was only one sure way to find out.

He had to see her again.

CHAPTER 5

With Crestpoint High's gymnasium under renovation, the school board called for everyone who wanted to attend the meeting on Saturday morning to gather on the beach. Most of the town's residents had come, crowding the sand while several board members stood in front of the growing assembly.

Annie found a spot toward the back with Hannah and their dad, worry knitting her brow as whispered rumors and murmured talk of changes coming to the school circulated the attendees.

"Do you think this is about all of the cuts?" Annie asked Hannah, who stood at her side.

"Most likely. It's all anyone has been talking about lately," Hannah replied within a sigh, reaching out to hook her arm through Annie's.

Annie chewed her bottom lip nervously, hearing that with recent slumps in tourism to Crestpoint Beach, businesses might have to shutter for a while or even file for bankruptcy if things didn't improve. She wasn't sure how true those claims were, but they still made her nervous about the future of her hometown.

She hadn't left all those years ago because she didn't like living in Crestpoint Beach. She'd gone to make something of herself, with the idea that one day she might be able to come back with a family of her own to raise. She couldn't imagine a better place to grow up than right here in her hometown. The thought of hard times and budget constraints carving away pieces of the place she loved put a knot of sadness in her chest.

"Everything will be okay," her father said, patting her arm and offering a calming smile. "Every town goes through growing pains now and then. Crestpoint Beach is no different."

Annie smiled back and nodded, figuring her father knew what he was talking about. Still, she couldn't help feeling protective of her hometown and its residents. She'd only been back for about a week, but each day it was becoming easier to sink deeper into her life here.

She and Hannah had scrubbed, dusted, and polished every corner of the old beach house, and although it was light on furniture in all but the essential rooms, Annie could move in anytime.

"Um…Annie," Hannah murmured beneath her breath, glancing past Annie's shoulder. "Act natural and be calm."

"Act natural, why? Do I have a bug on me?" She brushed at her shoulder, wondering if her sister knew that one sure way to make someone panic was to tell them to act natural and be calm. "Hannah, what's going on?"

"Nine o'clock. Noah Davis, heading right this way," Hannah whispered quickly in one breath before turning from Annie. She grabbed Frank's arm and led him away without a shred of subtlety, flashing a wink over her shoulder at Annie as they abandoned her to Noah.

Annie spun around and there he was, less than an arm's length between them. "Noah. Hi."

Her heart lurched up into her throat at the sight of him again. He looked casually handsome today in his light blue short-sleeve button-down, khaki shorts, and deck shoes. His muscled arms and toned calves were golden from living near the beach, and the hint of a beard shadowed his unshaved face. He smiled, revealing those twin dimples that used to make her knees a little weak. Still did, she was reluctant to admit.

"Hey, Annie. I saw you over here and just wanted to say hi."

She nodded, returning his warm smile. Now she wished she'd taken the time to pop in at the bungalow and freshen up after working at the beach house since before dawn. Her ponytail, pink tank top, black athletic shorts, and flip-flops had been fine for housecleaning, but she felt a little frumpy standing in front of him under the morning sun. It didn't help that Noah's ex-wife had shown up to the gathering looking like a fashion model in her crisp summer dress and heels.

"How are you settling in so far?" Noah asked, as his eyes swept over her briefly, lingering on her hair, before he smiled again.

He wasn't even touching her and her skin already felt like it was buzzing. She rubbed her hand over the arm closest to him, trying to get rid of the goosebumps that rose there. She needed to get a grip on herself. He was only being polite and neighborly. It was probably good that he was seeing her at her wilted, sweaty worst. Not that he should notice at all.

"I'm okay," she said. "I'm keeping busy. Hannah and I have actually been working on our grandparents' old beach house."

"Really? That's awesome. I always loved that beautiful house." He tilted his head. "You're not thinking about selling it, are you?"

"Never," she replied, horrified at the thought. "My dad and Hannah actually offered it to me to live in."

"So, you're sticking around?"

"For now," she said, wondering if the pleasure in his hazel eyes was only neighborly politeness too. "Um, so what have you been up to since I saw you last week? I mean, besides teaching."

It wasn't the first time she'd been curious about what he did in his free time. They used to do all sorts of things together, from taking silly photos of each other to catching hermit crabs to collecting cool rocks that they found in the woods. She missed having mindless hobbies like that. And someone to share them with.

Noah chuckled sheepishly as he rubbed at the back of his neck. "My buddy and I went fishing last night…but I didn't catch anything."

Annie didn't hold back her laugh. "Some things didn't change. Still not the best fisherman, huh?"

She couldn't help but tease him. One of their old high school dates had been an afternoon of fishing with a picnic dinner planned for afterward. Unfortunately, after a day amid the fishy smell of the pier it was hard to conjure up an appetite, but it was amusing to see Noah nearly throw himself over the railing after tossing his line out too hard.

"I don't think I'll ever be a trophy-winning angler at this point, but I still have fun. Maybe I should try a new hobby." Noah smirked, his eyes brightening as he gazed at her.

That look almost made her feel dizzy. She loved how the corners of his eyes crinkled when he smiled and how his grin went a little crooked when he was relaxed around someone. Small things like that stuck with her just as much as the big moments they had shared together. Back then, everything about Noah had meant the world to her.

"There's plenty of things to try around here. You could learn how to build sandcastles," Annie suggested, feeling something in her chest flutter. It was odd feeling like this again, and she couldn't help but feel guilty for the way her pulse sped up in front of a new man, especially when Derek had only been gone less than a year.

But Noah wasn't a new man. He was just…Noah.

He chuckled as he slid his hands into the pockets of his shorts. "You'd probably make a great sandcastle with your design experience. I remember you showing me some pretty impressive Barbie dollhouse rooms you put together in grade school."

"You remember that?"

"Sure, I do." His expression eased into a tentative seriousness. "I remember everything about those years, Annie."

That flutter in her chest was quickly turning into a swarm of butterflies. Her face felt hot and she knew she couldn't blame it all on the sun overhead. Inhaling a stabilizing breath, she schooled her face into a look of casual interest.

"So, you're a biology teacher? I would've guessed you might go into science or history." Annie recalled his love for learning in general. While he'd mused once in a while about teaching, his interests had been pretty split the last time that they had spoken about it. "What made up your mind toward science?"

"Well, I guess you probably had something to do with that decision."

"Me?"

"Yeah. We had so many great times exploring the beach or running around in the woods, looking at all the plants and animals and fossils we would find. Those times were more fun than reading books about the past."

Annie was astonished to realize she had a part to play in his chosen career path, especially after their breakup. Traces of him had stuck with her after she'd left, too. Whenever she smelled pizza in the dining hall at college she would think about how often they'd hung out together at Slice of Paradise to study or to unwind after they finished up hard tests. He was the first person she wanted to call whenever she had successes to celebrate or losses to get over. Whenever she needed encouragement to clear one more hurdle in her studies or in her career later on, it was Noah's voice she heard in the back of her mind, cheering her on, telling her there was nothing she couldn't achieve.

Noah's influence had guided her in more ways than she could count, even when there had been years and thousands of miles between them. She just never imagined she might have impacted him in the same way, particularly after he stood her up at the prom.

"I'm glad teaching worked out for you," she told him, trying to draw herself out of the seriousness of the moment. She needed to be able to talk to him about the past or to compliment him without being struck with memories and emotions she didn't know how to handle.

He nodded. "I heard you did great work over in Dallas. Your dad mentioned you had a lot of celebrities on your client list."

Annie shrugged modestly, unaccustomed to mentioning that part of her career to people. However, she was aware that rumors flowed like rivers here. Evidently, her own father had been the source of this particular tributary.

"It wasn't as impressive as it might sound. I designed the interior of a penthouse for a TV chef and a few homes for actors and athletes. They were mainly up-and-comers cashing the check from their first big break on a nice house with all the trimmings."

"That's still awesome," Noah said, a proud look on his face. "I remember when Mrs. King let you decorate her art classroom. She boasted to all of the other teachers for weeks because it looked so good."

It amazed her that he still remembered small instances like that. He had really paid attention to her. Despite the sting of the way things ended, she realized how comfortable she still felt around him all these years later. They were chatting like old friends again, and it felt good to settle back in with someone outside of her family.

"I can't believe that was all so long ago. Where did the time go?" Annie sighed wistfully as she shared a smile with him.

"Well, things feel more in place now that you're back," Noah replied.

The compliment, and the warm way he said it, made those butterflies stir all over again.

"I just wish these budget problems weren't happening," she said, desperate to deflect his attention. "It must be stressful for everyone at the school."

Annie turned her head as the school board members prepared to start the meeting. She couldn't miss Claudia and her silky auburn hair. She somehow looked ten times better than she did back in high school, having filled out her curves and the flawless features of her face even more. She could've been in pageants if she had wanted to. She still could, in fact.

Seeing Claudia now and knowing that she and Noah had once been married made a rush of insecurity course through Annie. She couldn't imagine trying to compete against Claudia Harrow then, or now. She glanced at Noah and found him studying her as if she was the only person on the beach with him.

"Yeah," he murmured, "the budget situation is kind of a nightmare. Especially for the kids, since it's the electives and extracurricular activities that are on the chopping block."

As he spoke, Claudia fluffed her hair and fixed her white blouse before stepping up to the front of the gathering, while the other four school board members stood behind her.

"Good morning, everyone. What a lovely Saturday. Thank you each and every one of you for coming out today," she announced in a cheery voice, prompting light applause from the crowd. "Now, I don't want to keep you too long, so let's just get right into it, shall we? As I'm sure you all have heard, we have been forced to make a few cost-saving cuts to various organizations and events this year."

While Claudia paused to allow a few worried murmurs to rumble and die down, Annie glanced over at Noah with a sympathetic look.

"Sorry about your science club. Hannah told me it's being cut."

The corner of Noah's mouth turned up into a faint smile. He leaned over to lightly bump his shoulder against hers in a silent motion of gratitude, one they used to use all of the time.

"The annual budget is stretched too thin, and the board has to focus on core programs first," Noah explained. "Unfortunately, that means after-school events and out-of-classroom teaching projects will be the first to go. Including my science club."

Annie wanted to offer some more words of support, but before she had a chance, Claudia began reading from a list of programs that were being added to the cuts.

"I'm sorry to say that effective immediately, the following events have been removed from the budget for the year: Chess Club's Tourney in the Park, the NHS Beach Clean-up Crew field trip to Turtle Island, Crestpoint High's prom..."

A spattering of groans and boos echoed after each doomed event was named, but the announcement of prom being canceled prompted emotional cries and wails of dismay from all over the crowd.

Annie's eyes followed the sound of the most anguished protest to its source, spotting Noah's daughter looking distraught with a few of her friends. Annie felt a sharp pang in her chest at Lainey's expression.

"The other board members and I are very sorry," Claudia said, projecting her voice above the complaints. "I understand everyone is disappointed, but I assure you, these cuts are necessary. Thank you for your time today."

Claudia finished up her speech before waving her hand as she stepped back without taking questions or addressing the obvious disgruntlement left in her wake. Voices filled the beach as people fretted over their own programs being cut or events they were looking forward to being canceled.

Noah exhaled sharply, his brows knit. "I can't believe they're cutting prom, of all things. Claudia knew how much Lainey was looking forward to going. The poor girl's probably devastated."

Annie rested her hand on his bicep. "I'm sorry, Noah."

He shook his head. "I have to find a way to fix this.

Lainey's having a tough enough time with her mother this year as it is. She deserves to have at least one good thing happen that she doesn't have to stress about."

It was interesting seeing Noah as a father. Annie always expected him to be a good one, but he was acting like a superhero right now with his determination to try to save prom for his daughter. It was a devotion that she wished he'd shown toward their own prom, but she shoved those thoughts away. Things were different now. They were different people, and he was a great dad. He had her admiration for that fact alone.

"What are you going to do?" Annie asked him, wondering if he had a plan in mind. It was likely to be a hard task for him to get Claudia to change her mind on her decision or persuade the school board to reconsider.

Noah gazed through the crowd at his daughter, who was in a comfort circle with her friends. "I don't know what I'll do yet, but I'm going to figure something out."

Despite not having met Lainey, Annie found herself agreeing with him. She did deserve a great prom. If Annie had a daughter she'd want her to be able to have the night of her life with a beautiful dress, a cute date, and great friends. In fact, she wanted Noah's daughter to have all of that, too.

"Maybe I could help you. If you want, that is," Annie offered, figuring she had the extra time on her hands outside of working on the beach house and looking after her dad. Besides, it would help her get to know Noah better and maybe allow her to get used to being around him again. She didn't know how much longer she could take the blushing and butterflies she constantly felt around him.

He grinned at her. "Really? That would be amazing. Maybe we can think of a way to raise some money for the prom and a few of the other things that are getting cut, or maybe we can find other places for the board to make adjustments instead."

Annie smiled and nodded, thinking that those ideas were great places to start. There was a solution somewhere. They just needed to find it together.

CHAPTER 6

*S*eagulls cackled wildly outside Coast Coffeehouse as Noah walked up to the entrance of the café.

After getting Annie's number at Saturday's meeting, they had made a plan to meet up the following day at the popular beachside hangout and start brainstorming ideas. Noah opened the front door, making the entrance bell jingle as he stepped inside.

At ten in the morning, a little while after the Sunday breakfast rush, it was fairly quiet for the moment. Because Coast Coffeehouse bordered the beach, its front wall of rectangular windows took full advantage of the view, showing off the beauty of the sparkling waves and glistening sand. The interior of the café was full of cozy, round wooden tables, local artists' paintings along the walls, an ordering counter toward the back corner, and golden light bulbs hanging from the ceiling.

Noah spotted Annie immediately as though his eyes were drawn to hers in a magnetic pull he couldn't fight. He held his hand up in greeting, motioning to her that he would be there in a moment.

Annie smiled back and nodded from a table near one of the windows. She held a frothy cup of cappuccino close to her chest, turning her head to look out at the water.

Noah ordered a black coffee, unable to keep his eyes from straying Annie's way as he waited for his order. She looked good today in a sunny yellow T-shirt, white shorts, and sandals, with her blonde hair swept back in a loose ponytail. He loved it when she wore her hair like that because it allowed him to drink in all of the soft features of her face.

"Here you go, Mr. Davis," The barista, a student of his from four years ago, placed the steaming paper coffee cup in front of him on the counter.

"Thanks, Kendra."

The young woman gave him a sad smile. "I heard about the budget cuts. How awful of them to cut the prom. The whole town's talking about it."

Noah nodded. "I know. Hopefully, things will start looking up soon."

He grabbed his coffee and turned to walk over to Annie, feeling a lightness in his stomach as he approached her table. He had to remind himself she wasn't meeting him for any other reason than to offer her help in trying to solve the funding problems with the school programs. His problems, not Annie's. He didn't know if they'd be able to do anything to change the outcome, but the fact that she had volunteered her support was more than he could ask for.

It was more than he rightfully deserved, after the terrible way he'd treated her all those years ago. If he needed a reminder to keep things casual and professional with her, the anguish he'd caused her was reason enough.

"Hi," he said, taking the chair across from her. "Thanks again for meeting me to try to help with all of this. Morale at the school was already about as low as I've ever seen. I can only imagine what it'll be like starting tomorrow. It's hard enough getting juniors and seniors to focus in class. Now, it's nearly impossible because they don't have a prom to look forward to."

Annie gave him a sympathetic look. "I'm sorry to hear that. I can kind of understand the reaction, though. Can't you? When you're that age, things like prom and graduation loom as big as your wedding day or the birth of your first child. Those last couple years of high school are everything to a teenager."

Her voice faded off and she took a sip of her cappuccino. Silence fell for a few long moments. Noah didn't have to guess about her sudden quiet after her comment. She had been that excited about her prom, too. It was practically all she talked about in the weeks leading up to the dance. Then he ruined it for her by not showing up.

Noah cleared his throat. "I thought of some ideas," he said, figuring his failing with her was a topic that they could address later. They had to focus on the present and the future before they worked on their past. He couldn't change what he'd done to her. However, he was in control of how he treated Annie now.

She set her cup down on its saucer. "Oh, yeah? Let me hear what you've got."

He set his tablet on the table between them and opened a spreadsheet that contained a dozen or so programs that weren't as popular as his science club or the prom. He swiveled the display so Annie could read it.

"We can try to convince the board to make cuts elsewhere,"

he told her as she studied his list, "but that might be hard since everything matters to someone in some way, you know? Who are we to decide what's important and what's not?"

The situation was tough all around, and he didn't want to be like Claudia and the board. He didn't want to decide what deserved to stay and what needed to go. Noah saw worth in everything, the same way he saw something special in each of his students.

Annie glanced up at him as if she could sense the depth of his conflict. Knowing her, she probably did.

"You're right," she said. "Even if the board did want to listen to us, we shouldn't put a bullseye on anyone else's program. After all, we didn't like that they cut things like prom because it's only a social event to them, or the beach clean-up team because they're a small group doing limited work. Everyone's always pulled together in this town. That's what makes Crestpoint Beach so special."

Noah could tell she was glad to be back in town, and, selfishly, he was incredibly happy that she was back as well. He was beginning to see some of the determined, passionate Annie he used to know and love so well. He hadn't realized just how deeply he'd missed her all these years.

He took a drink of his coffee. "Maybe money can be borrowed from other departments that are doing fine," he suggested. "The money could be more evenly distributed that way."

Annie responded with a mild shrug. "That's an option, if you really think the board would consider it. Another would be to try to raise some money."

"That might be easier said than done. Folks around here are struggling a bit these days. We still get the snowbirds and the seasonal tourism booms every year, but things get lean during the lulls," he pointed out. "Do you have any thoughts for fund-raising ideas?"

She brought her cup to her lips, a pensive look in her pretty blue eyes. "Nothing solid right now, but I'm sure we can come up with something if we put our heads together. We always did in the past, right?"

"Yeah, we did," he said, his voice lowering as he stared at her across the small table.

Now that he was really looking at her again, he could see she was carrying a sadness inside her despite the brightness of her outlook on life or the earnest way she tackled every problem in front of her.

She was still hurting after the loss of her husband, yet here she was throwing herself into his troubles.

"I'm here for you if you ever want to talk about it."

He didn't have to spell out what he meant for Annie. She glanced down and nodded, her forehead pinching. "Sometimes, it still doesn't feel real that he's gone."

"I'm sorry, Annie. I heard about the accident."

She glanced up again, clearly struggling to collect herself. "Derek loved riding his motorcycle. He used to take me with him, and we'd ride an hour or so out of Dallas and spend the day exploring some of the cute towns and festivals along the way. It was something we loved doing together."

"Sounds like fun," Noah said, finding it easy to picture Annie enjoying that kind of a day, even if the idea of her on the back of a motorcycle didn't seem to fit the more conservative side of her that he had known.

She grew a little quiet, idling tracing her finger around the rim of her cup. "I was supposed to be with him that day, Noah."

He frowned, his heart all but seizing in his chest. "What do you mean?"

"The day of Derek's accident. We were supposed to ride together to Grapevine to meet up with one of his clients, but the weather reports called for possible rain and thunderstorms. I didn't think it was safe to take the bike, but Derek had a new one and he wanted to show it off to his client." Annie lifted her shoulder in a faint shrug and slowly shook her head. "I refused to go unless we took the car instead. So, Derek left without me."

Noah drew back, horrified to think she might have been lost that day, too.

He was also angry that her husband would have pressured her to take an irresponsible risk like that with him.

"Annie...as awful as Derek's passing must have been for you, I am so relieved that you didn't go with him that day."

He wished that he could reach out and take her hand, to offer her some comfort, but he stopped himself. It wasn't his place to touch her. She hadn't asked for his comfort, and he wasn't going to force it on her, least of all when she was looking so vulnerable.

"I'm sorry you had to face that kind of pain alone," he murmured. "Does your father know what you just told me? Or Hannah?"

She shook her head. "Just you. I've felt too guilty to tell anyone else."

It struck him deep that she would confide in him. Noah would've taken her pain away right then if he could. However, he didn't have the power to do that. All he could do was try to guide her through it until it didn't hurt so bad.

As he looked at her, Noah sent up a silent prayer of thanks for the fact that she was sitting in front of him today.

"You shouldn't feel guilty for a minute," he told her gently. "It was Derek's decision to ride that day. You had every right to say no."

"Thank you for saying that," she whispered. "I just feel like I let him down when I refused to go with him. He was upset when he left."

"Hey," Noah said, urging her to meet his gaze. "Not your fault, okay?"

She stared at him for a moment, then gave him a shaky nod.

Noah gripped his coffee cup a little tighter to keep himself from reaching out to her. Whether she needed a shoulder to cry on or someone to distract her for a little while, he would do anything to make her feel at least a little better. "I'm here for you if you need anything, Annie. I mean that."

"Just like old times," she said, a sad smile edging her lips.

That hint of a smile seemed to take some of the heaviness out of the air around them. Her grief and guilt couldn't be dissolved so easily, but in time he hoped she'd move past all of the difficult emotions she'd brought home with her from Dallas.

Until then, Noah intended to be the friend she used to lean on. It only seemed fair, since she had been the only thing that got him through the problems and pain of his own past.

"Seems so long ago, doesn't it?" he asked. "You were basically my whole childhood."

It was true. Noah chuckled warmly, realizing that a majority of his fondest memories during that time involved her. They spent so much time together, whether they were in classes together at school, hanging out on the weekends, or going out on dates when they were older. They were inseparable from third grade forward.

"We did have fun," she said, her mood brightening. "I'll never forget that little date we had in the woods our sophomore year, when we ended up getting lost for half a day."

Noah remembered, too. Weeks before that day, he had found a nice clearing deep in the woods on one of his solo exploring adventures. He thought that it was a perfect spot for a picnic date with Annie, so he asked her out, prepared a whole basket of sandwiches, chips, and bottles of lemonade, then made her hoof out to the woods with him. Unfortunately, since he had only been to the spot once before, he ended up getting them lost in the thick of the woods with no phones to call for help.

He chuckled to recall the ordeal. "I think we were stranded for about six hours. I was ready to go full-on caveman to make sure that we survived, right down to making fire with sticks and eating bugs."

She laughed behind her hand. "At least we had plenty of food. I remember those turkey sandwiches you made for us were pretty great."

"I still make a pretty good sandwich," he boasted with a shrug.

"You always made food for me. I thought it was one of the most romantic things ever."

"I considered it necessity. After my parents divorced and my dad left when I was thirteen, my mom started working three jobs to make ends meet for us. I never wanted to ask her for anything when she was already doing so much, so I learned to cook for both of us. Sandwiches were my culinary training wheels."

Annie smiled. "Well, you excelled at it."

"Let me know if you ever want me to test a recipe on you."

"Careful, I might take you up on that," she said. "I've been spending so much time working on the beach house and pitching in with Dad, sometimes I forget to eat."

"That's not good," Noah quipped. "I keep meaning to ask you how it's going over at the beach house."

"It's going well, but Hannah and I have a long way to go on it yet." She pushed her empty cup aside. "I could give you a quick tour now if you want."

"Yeah? I'd like that," Noah replied with an enthusiastic nod, feeling honored that she was letting him see her work before she was done with it.

They cleared their table and headed out to make the short trek down the beach toward the house.

"Not all of my furniture has come in yet, but I'm trying not to deplete my savings all in one fell swoop. Besides, I'm still adding new touches and rethinking some things, so what you see today may be completely rearranged the next time," Annie warned him as they walked together, the waves crashing in the distance as seagulls glided through the air above their heads.

Noah merely smiled as he listened to her, fascinated just to hear her talk about her work. He knew she was creative and artistic when they were growing up, but it wasn't until high school that she began talking seriously about pursuing a career in interior design.

"I'll bet it's already nearly perfect," Noah assured her as they stopped in front of the large light-blue beach house. He followed her up the steps to the front door, waiting for her to unlock it before trailing her inside.

"Oh, wow. It's awesome." Noah took everything in, his eyes sweeping over a fresh coat of soothing, pale blue paint on the walls and crisp white trim around all of the many windows facing the water. The living area was open concept and airy, furnished with casual, comfortable looking couches and club chairs, and a light-patterned, woven rug on the floor. There wasn't a lot of furniture in the place, but on the whole the vibe of the house was warm and inviting, yet classic. He could see Annie's personal touch in every piece and color and arrangement everywhere he looked.

He spotted a bit of Hannah, too. A collection of recently painted seashells lay out to dry on some newspapers that were spread out atop a wood dining table.

"Come on," Annie said. "Let me show you the upstairs, too."

He followed her up the polished and painted staircase to the second floor, where three of the six bedrooms were, each with their own adjoining bathroom. Noah recalled there were two more bedrooms on the first floor with a shared bathroom between them, and still another bedroom and bathroom on the third floor of the grand old Victorian.

"I forgot how massive this place is," he said as they paused outside one of the freshly redesigned bedrooms.

Annie nodded. "Yeah, it's much too big for me all by myself. But I have to admit, I'm really excited to be able to design so many rooms."

"I can tell you are." Finding it impossible not to share her enthusiasm, he stepped into the cozy bedroom with its creamy, seafoam-colored walls and frothy bedding. Outside the romantic bay window overlooking the beach, the blue-green water glittered under the sunlight.

"We're nowhere near finished," Annie said, "but I think it's coming along nicely."

There was a hint of pride in her tone that had Noah smiling when he looked at her.

"It's amazing, Annie. I can't imagine how much thought

and skill it takes to make a big, lonely house feel like a home, but you're doing it."

He hadn't realized they were standing less than a foot away from each other until that moment. The nearness to her made his heart speed up, and sent a buzz of awareness racing over his skin.

"It's been really therapeutic for me," Annie murmured, her voice dropping down a degree quieter as her eyes met his.

Noah swallowed, his throat suddenly going dry. "I'm glad to hear that." He broke her stare, desperate to look at anything other than the gorgeous blue pools of her eyes. His attention snagged on a delicate black lash that rested on the curve of her pinkening cheek. "You, um, you've got an eyelash right here…"

He could feel Annie's gaze on his as he lightly brushed his fingertips along her cheek to sweep the eyelash away, her breath hitching slightly at the touch.

Noah knew his hand was shaking a bit, but he couldn't help it. He hadn't touched her in years, and her skin felt so perfect and soft beneath his fingertips. He drew his hand away once the eyelash was gone, and found her eyes still locked on him.

He wanted to touch her cheek again. What he really wanted to do was lift her chin and press a kiss to her parted lips, just to see if her mouth was as soft and sweet as he remembered.

Everything he felt for her came flooding back as he gazed at her now.

He wasn't over her at all.

Had he ever really gotten over Annie Taylor?

She drew in a sharp breath, then took a step away from him. "Anyway, working on the house has been more of a gift than anyone could know. It's given me something constructive to focus on, instead of…everything else."

Noah shoved his hands into his pockets, if only to keep them away from her. The way she backed away and now began heading out of the room seemed to be a good indicator that he had overstepped his bounds with even that innocent brush of his fingertips on her cheek.

She dutifully led him through the rest of the house, pointing out the changes she'd made and telling him about the ones she hoped to implement soon. He nodded and listened with genuine interest, but inside he was practically kicking himself for ruining what he thought had been the start of their rekindled friendship.

They didn't get as close to each other after that bungled touch. Noah didn't want to push it since Annie seemed a bit tense now. He hoped he hadn't crossed a line.

Once they made their way back down to the main floor, Noah figured it was past time for him to leave.

"Well, I should get going. It's my week with Lainey, and I need to pick her up from Claudia's house soon. Thank you for showing me the beach house, Annie. It looks incredible."

"Thanks." Her smile seemed tentative. "I'm sure you'll be hearing more about it, now that we're working together on ideas for fundraising for the school."

"Right," he said, hoping he didn't appear as awkward as he felt around her now.

She walked with him to the door and stepped out onto the veranda beside him. "When should we plan to meet again?"

He ran a hand through his hair and blew out a sigh. "I'll be teaching all week, so my next available day might not be until Saturday. Or Sunday, since I'll have Lainey with me until then."

"I don't mind if you bring Lainey. She might have some good ideas, too."

He smiled, surprised she would offer to include his daughter. Then again, this was Annie. Her kindness should never come as a surprise. "Okay, Saturday, it is."

He knew he should just turn around and get off the veranda as fast as possible, but the instinct to be near Annie got the best of him and he stepped toward her and gave her a quick hug. Once he had his arms around her, he felt even more awkward about it, so before releasing her, he lamely patted her on the back the way he would an elderly neighbor or one of the ladies at church.

"Goodbye, Annie."

The look on her face said she felt as uncomfortable as he did now.

Great. He was doing a fantastic job here.

Before he could make things any worse, he jogged down the steps to the sand then walked briskly back to the street where he'd parked outside the coffeehouse.

CHAPTER 7

Annie didn't hear from Noah at all in the week after she'd invited him to see the beach house. She knew he was likely busy with teaching and handling the fallout from last Saturday's announcement about deeper cuts at school, but she couldn't help feeling that he might be avoiding her, too.

Try as she might, she'd been unable to stop reliving the moment he touched her while she had been showing him around the house. It hadn't been anything at all, just him brushing an eyelash off her cheek, but it had sent her heart on a wild gallop. It made her think he might have wanted to kiss her.

She wasn't sure how to feel about it at the time. Anticipation and surprise had warred with guilt as she held her breath and stared into Noah's warm hazel eyes. In the end, confusion won the battle of her emotions and she'd drawn away from him.

A full week later, she was still confused about what she was feeling for Noah. She had no idea what to think about his feelings for her, either. That stiff embrace he'd given her before he left seemed to make it fairly clear that he meant to keep things casual between them. Besides that, he could hardly seem to get away from her fast enough, practically bolting out of the house after she'd concluded her brief tour with him.

It was for the best, anyway. He had plenty of personal issues to deal with and so did she. If they could be friends again and also work something out to help the Crestpoint High kids, that was enough for her.

"Here's your omelet and toast, Dad," she said, stepping out of the bungalow's galley kitchen with her father's breakfast.

Although she'd already moved into one of the bedrooms at the beach house, she made a point of checking in with her father a couple times a day. Today, since Hannah was working a morning shift at the gift shop, Annie came early to make breakfast.

She set the plate down on her father's tray standing beside his recliner, then went back to fetch his juice and utensils. He was peering at the food skeptically when she returned.

"What's the green stuff in my eggs?"

"Kale. It's good for you."

He grunted. "And what happened to my cinnamon-and-raisin toast?"

Annie laughed and shook her head. "I made you sprouted whole grain today instead. Give it a try, I think you'll like it."

He harumphed, but there was a twinkle in his eyes as he poked at the food with his fork. "Is this what they eat in Dallas?"

She nodded, smiling. "It's also what you're going to be eating a bit more of right here at home."

"Hannah doesn't make me eat this healthy stuff," he groused lightheartedly.

Annie stole one of the blueberries from his plate and popped it into her mouth. "Hannah and I have agreed it's time for you to make a few changes in your diet and also get out of the house more often."

"Ah, you two have been colluding behind my back, is that it?"

"You bet we have."

He chuckled. "Guess I'll have to get used to the idea of being outnumbered and outfoxed by my clever girls."

Annie laughed, leaning down to kiss his whiskered cheek. Her phone rang at the same time, vibrating on the kitchen counter where she'd left it while she cooked. She ran to pick up the call, smiling when she saw who it was.

"Hi, Noah."

"Good morning. Hope I'm not calling too early."

"Nope. I just made a quick breakfast for Dad, then I was about to head over to the beach house to get a little work in. What's up?"

He paused. "I know we were planning to get together this afternoon to discuss fundraising ideas, but I wonder if you'd be willing to do me a favor first. Lainey and me, actually."

Her curiosity perked up. "Sure. What can I do?"

"I've been promising her a new desk for her room at my place for a couple of months now. I was wondering if you wouldn't mind meeting us at Seaside Design and helping her pick something out."

"I'd be happy to. When would you like to meet up?"

"We're on our way there now, if you're free."

The only thing she had waiting for her was a morning of work at the beach house, and that would still be waiting for her whenever she got there. "Sounds good," she said. "I'll walk over right after we hang up."

"That's great." She could almost hear his smile in his deep voice. "Thanks, Annie. I know Lainey will enjoy meeting you."

"I'm looking forward to meeting her, too."

Annie ended the call and let her dad know her plans. Then she hurried to the bathroom to fix her unbound hair and freshen up. On impulse, she quickly changed out of her T-shirt and denim shorts, tossing a simple, floral-patterned skater dress over her head.

"Okay, Dad, I'm off."

He saluted her with his fork, a mouthful of omelet in his mouth. "Have fun, sweetheart."

With her purse in hand and a pair of sandals on her feet, she headed out into the morning sunshine.

Noah was just pulling up to the front of the store when Annie arrived on foot. She waved at him and Lainey as he parked his black Jeep Cherokee in one of the open spots.

"Lainey, this is Annie. We went to high school together," Noah said, once they were all standing outside the door to Seaside Design.

"I saw you at the pizza place that one day," Lainey said, shooting her father a cryptic look. "Dad says you two went to school here together."

"Yes, we did. From elementary school through senior high," Annie replied, returning the girl's dimpled smile. Lainey looked so much like her father, it nearly took Annie's breath away. "I hear you're in the market for a new desk."

She nodded. "My dad says you're really good with decorating and stuff. Do you think you can help me find something cool? Maybe some decorations for my room, too?"

"I'm sure we'll find lots of things you'll like. My friend,

Zoe, works here and I'll bet she has a great selection of desks that we can check out."

Annie gestured for them to follow her inside of the furniture store. She called out to Zoe, prompting the younger girl to come bounding toward them from the back of the store.

"Hi, Annie! Nice to see you again. And you brought guests."

Zoe greeted Annie with a hug. Annie and Hannah had been spending a lot of time in the store, and as a result, the three of them had become a tight-knit group of friends.

"Zoe, this is Noah and his daughter, Lainey." After Zoe and Noah shook hands, Annie went on. "We're on a quest for a nice desk for Lainey and maybe some other bedroom items and accents."

"You came to the right place. We have some new things that just arrived," Zoe replied as she led them across the floor toward a display full of desks for work or school.

"You seem a bit alternative and avant-garde to me," Annie murmured as she gazed at Lainey, taking a cue from her black Converse sneakers, distressed skinny jeans, and loose-fitting Andy Warhol T-shirt. She wanted to find a piece that matched Lainey's personality and style, which automatically ruled out the selection of fussy desks painted in pastel colors.

"Yeah, avant-garde," Lainey agreed with a wry smile. "That's the kind of stuff I like. I mean, I like cute things, too. I guess I like a mish-mash of styles. Does that make sense?"

"Sure. There are no hard rules when it comes to defining your own personal style."

Annie suspected Lainey was at the stage when she had no idea what to do next with her life. Annie had been there herself many times, most recently after Derek's accident. For a while, she felt like she was floating in space with nothing to anchor her. She should have known she'd find her grounding back home in Crestpoint Beach. Every day she was there, she felt herself settling in more and more.

"I know that the power of choice is daunting," she told Lainey. "You'll learn a lot about yourself in the process. Have a look at these desks. Do any of them call out to you?"

Lainey tapped her chin thoughtfully as her eyes swept over the three remaining desks of varying color and design. Her eyes continually shifted to the right, prompting her to point to a sleek black desk with white trim and knobs.

"I like that one."

Zoe nodded at Annie, smiling. "That's a great choice. Not only does it look cool, but it also has extra deep drawer space for any school supplies you need to store." She grabbed one of the knobs to pull the drawer out so Lainey could peek inside.

While the two of them talked about the desk and Zoe guided Lainey to another section of the display to point out other pieces that complemented it, Annie glanced at Noah and found him smiling at her.

"Thank you for doing this," he said. "I haven't seen my daughter so enthused about anything in a long time."

"My pleasure," Annie replied, meaning it wholeheartedly.

She liked Lainey, and it warmed her to see what Noah was like as a father. She'd always known he'd be a patient, caring parent. There was a time when Annie had truly believed they would be raising a family of their own. More than just believed it, she'd yearned for it.

Now, she would have to settle for seeing his happiness with Lainey. As for her own prospects of having children, she hadn't totally given up hope, even at thirty-five. Feeling her heart squeeze as she watched Noah and Lainey together put a pang of guilt in her when she thought of Derek and the fact that he'd never had the opportunity to be a father.

"There is another slight change in our plans today," Noah said, his quiet voice pulling her out of her dark thoughts.

"Okay. What happened?"

"Claudia," he replied. "She wants me to drop Lainey at her house today instead of tomorrow. I know you were open to having Lainey weigh in with some ideas, but she's due at Claudia's in about an hour."

"That's all right. If you'd rather reschedule our brainstorming session—"

"Actually, I had another thought." He hesitated, studying her for a moment. "Why don't you come with us?"

"To Claudia's house?" Annie almost sputtered the words.

He nodded. "Maybe we can persuade her to reconsider, or at least hear us out about alternatives for cutting the kids' prom."

Annie swallowed. "I don't know, Noah…"

He held up his hands. "It's okay. You don't have to go. I should probably have that conversation with her alone, anyway."

"How do you think that will go?"

He smirked. "About as well as it'll go if you're with me. But this isn't your battle to fight. It's mine. I'm sorry I mentioned it, Annie."

"I didn't actually say no yet." She stared up at him, trying to decide if she had the courage to get in the middle of a conflict between him and his ex-wife.

Of course, the conflict they were discussing was more about Crestpoint High than Noah and Claudia's personal differences. When it came to doing things for the good of her hometown and its residents, Annie was all in.

"If you think she'll listen to what we have to say, then yes. I'll be glad to go with you today."

Surprise filled his gaze. "You're sure?"

She nodded, feeling his warm regard linger on her as Lainey hurried back to them, excitement gleaming in her eyes.

"Can I really get that desk for my room, Dad? It's kind of expensive."

He chuckled, cupping Lainey's head in his broad palm. "You let me worry about that. If you want it, it's yours, kiddo."

She let out a happy squeal and dashed back over for another look at the furniture. When Zoe drifted toward them, Noah asked her quietly, "Do you have any accessories to go with it? I'd like to add a few items to our order and surprise Lainey with them."

"Of course," Zoe said. "There's a catalog for this set right next to the register. I had a feeling you might be interested, so I've already opened it to the relevant page for you while your daughter was busy browsing other things. Just jot down the items you want on the sheet of paper I set out on the counter and I'll take care of everything."

He grinned. "Thank you."

As soon as he was out of earshot, Zoe turned to Annie with an intrigued look on her face.

"Whoa, he's good looking, huh? Single, too, based on the absence of a ring on his hand."

Annie shrugged. "Mm-hm."

Zoe's eyes widened and she dropped her voice to a whisper. "You're blushing."

"No, I'm not. Am I?" Annie brought her fingers to her face and groaned to feel fire in her cheeks. She waved her hand in front of her, both to generate some much-needed coolness and to try to dismiss Zoe's curiosity. "It's just warm in here."

Zoe arched her brows. "Is there something going on between you two?"

"What? No." Although she considered Zoe a friend, she hadn't yet divulged her past history with Noah. Nor was she ready to do that now, when both he and his daughter were under the same roof with them. "Noah and I went to school together here in Crestpoint Beach. We're just old friends."

"I'm not getting a 'just old friends' vibe," Zoe said. "Especially not from him. Have you noticed the way he looks at you?"

Annie frowned. She didn't want to think about the way he looked at her, or the way she felt when she was looking at him. She wasn't ready to unpack her old feelings about Noah, let alone acknowledge any of the new ones that were blossoming inside her.

"We're friends, that's all," she murmured, uncertain who she needed to convince more: her friend, or herself. "Besides, I'm not ready for anything more than that."

Zoe pressed her lips together, sympathy in her eyes. "I'm sorry. I didn't mean to make light of your situation—"

"You didn't, and it's okay," Annie assured her.

While they were talking, Lainey had moved on to a display of desk accessories ranging from college sports themed wastebaskets to kitschy marine life staplers and everything in between.

She pivoted to look at Annie, holding up a pair of animal character tape dispensers. "Which one do you think I should get? The dolphin or the alligator?"

Annie tilted her head as she considered them. "Dolphin, no question."

"That's what I was thinking too," Lainey said, grinning.

She returned the alligator to its display, then skipped over to where Noah was discreetly folding the sheet of paper Zoe had left for him to fill out. Lainey chattered animatedly with her dad as Zoe and Annie walked over to join them at the register.

All told, it took close to an hour before they had checked out and scheduled the desk delivery. After saying goodbye to Zoe, the three of them walked out together to Noah's Jeep.

As they reached the vehicle, Lainey surprised Annie by stepping in and giving her a hug. "Thank you for helping me with my desk and stuff, Annie."

"You're welcome. It was fun."

Lainey nodded, her smile beaming. "Will I see you again sometime?"

"Actually," Noah interjected, "Annie and I have some planning to do about the school funding, so I've asked her to come with us to drop you off at your mom's now."

"Oh. That's cool." Lainey's gaze bounced between them, a curious look lighting in her hazel eyes that were so much like Noah's. "I'll hop in back, so Annie can sit next to you up front, Dad."

Noah's answering smile said he was picking up the same budding matchmaker signals in his daughter that Annie was.

They all climbed into the vehicle and made the short drive to Claudia's house on the edge of town. Lainey's cheery mood dimmed the closer they got to the elegant two-story brick home with white pillars and white-framed windows. Noah parked on the sloped concrete driveway and turned off the ignition.

"You're sure you're okay with this?"

Annie nodded, taking a fortifying breath. "I'm fine with it, if you are."

He smiled. "Let's go."

They trailed after Lainey to the soaring entrance of the large home. Before they had even reached the last step to the door, the polished wood panel swung open and Claudia stood there, looking flawless in a pair of tailored cream slacks and a matching top. Annie felt a sense of relief that she'd taken the time to put on a summer dress instead of showing up in her shorts and T-shirt.

Although the way Claudia's gaze lit on her in surprise and disapproval, Annie might as well have been standing in front of her wearing a burlap sack.

Claudia's eyes slid to Noah with even colder regard. "What's this about?"

"Hi to you, too, Mom," Lainey grumbled as she stepped past her mother into the house.

Noah and Annie remained on the porch. "Claudia, you may remember Annie Taylor from high school. She was in our graduating class."

"I know who she is." Claudia seemed to draw herself a little straighter, her expression growing sharper and guarded, as if she were the one feeling the most awkward with this impromptu visit. "Noah told me about you a long time ago. I know the two of you were…friendly…in school."

Uncomfortable heat washed into Annie's face at the mild insinuation, but she smiled pleasantly and held out her hand. "My name is Annie Collins now."

Claudia reached out and gave her a brief handshake before her cool gaze flicked back to Noah. "What are you doing here? And why was my daughter with the two of you together?"

"Our daughter," he clarified firmly. "I asked Annie to help advise me on a new desk for Lainey's room back at my place."

Claudia's chin rose a notch. "I assume that didn't require bringing your friend to my house unannounced."

"Mom!" Lainey gasped from behind her in the foyer. "Don't be so rude. Annie's super nice."

Claudia flinched at her daughter's rebuke, but held her ground in the open space of the door. "Why are you here?"

Noah held her stare. "We want to talk with you about the school budget cuts and discuss some possible alternatives."

Annie nodded. "I apologize that we're springing this on you without any notice, Claudia, but the prom in particular can't wait. If we're going to look for ways to salvage it, we need to put them into action as soon as possible."

Lainey popped up next to her mother in the doorway. "Can't you at least hear what they have to say, Mom? Please?"

Claudia sighed heavily before waving her hand to motion for them to come inside. She looked over at Lainey, who leaned against the foyer wall.

"Lainey, why don't you head up to your room and let the grown-ups talk?"

"I'd rather stay and listen. This affects me, too."

Annie noticed Noah trying to conceal a proud smile as Claudia gestured for them all to follow her into the living room. They took their seats, Annie and Noah on each end of a sofa, Lainey slouched on a loveseat, and Claudia perched primly on the edge of a Queen Anne chair.

Annie glanced at Noah, silently offering to get things started.

"Claudia, we recognize that the school needs to be careful with its money, but it's also important that we don't lose the spirit of fun and community that's always been part of Crestpoint High. That's what makes the school and this town so special."

Noah nodded, picking up where she left off, just like he used to do. "Annie's right. Programs like the after-school clubs and the beach clean-up crew not only encourage the students to think outside the box of basic studies, but they also give them a means of getting actively involved in their community and help them develop an appreciation for their surroundings. You may think those kinds of programs are frivolous, but they mean a lot to the kids. Everyone's been feeling pretty deflated since the things they love have gone under the ax."

Annie jumped in again, building off his energy. "Losing the clubs and activities is a disappointment, for sure. Losing the prom means taking away the students' biggest celebration of the year. For the seniors, it's their last chance to have fun with friends they might not see again for years once college and adulthood pulls them in different directions. Some of them might not reconnect ever again."

"Hurt feelings don't repair budgets. We need to save money, which means cutting down on unnecessary spending. The extracurricular activities and dances use up too much of the money that could be put to better, more practical, use elsewhere," Claudia explained with a shake of her head.

Noah leaned forward, propping his forearms on his knees. "Are there any departments that are overachieving this year? Maybe the wealth could be spread around this year to keep things afloat. Most of what you're cutting is needed or makes the money back. Kids buy prom tickets and photo packages."

"Not to mention all of the local businesses that benefit as well," Annie added. "Prom means tuxedo rentals, limousine services, catering. Claudia, I'll bet Harrow's Cove sells dozens of formal gowns and cocktail dresses around prom season."

"That's beside the point." Claudia's mouth pursed, and she waved her hand dismissively. "I will not take money away from a successful department in order to prop up weaker ones. It doesn't work like that. Also, on the whole, the prom costs more money than what is made back. The school has to pay for the venue, the music, refreshments, lights, decorations, among other things. It's just not worth the money that's spent on it."

Lainey sat up. "It is worth it, Mom. My friends and I have wanted to go to prom since freshman year. Now, everyone hates me because of you."

Claudia flinched as if she'd been slapped. It took a moment before she spoke again. "You should be worrying about scholarships and figuring out what you want to do with your life, not fretting over silly things like a dance, or what other people think of you."

"Your mom is right," Annie said gently, looking from Lainey to Claudia. "I agree with you on a lot of those points, Claudia, but don't you also agree that kids should be allowed to have some fun before they have to worry about all of the adult concerns waiting for them after graduation?"

She hoped to reduce the tension in the room, but the bewildered look on Claudia's face said she did otherwise.

"Fun doesn't win scholarships. Fun doesn't guarantee a career or a future that will keep her from living on the street. If you're going to give advice, it better be useful." Claudia stood up. "I care about Lainey's future. I care about the school and this town's future, and I'm doing what I can to guarantee the success of all those things, whether you and my ex-husband like my methods or not. Since it's clear that you don't, it's probably best that we end this conversation."

She sailed out of the room, leaving Annie feeling as if she'd only made things worse. Noah went over to Lainey and gave her a long hug and some murmured words of encouragement before he walked back to Annie.

"I'm so sorry," she said, shaking her head. "I shouldn't have come."

"You were great," he assured her, wrapping his arm around her shoulders. "Maybe she'll come around in time."

As soon as Noah released her, Lainey came over and hugged her too. "Thanks for sticking up for me, Annie."

Annie stroked her fingers over the girl's soft brown hair. "I hope your mom won't be mad at you for what I said."

"Nah, she'll get over it. She always does, eventually." Lainey rolled her eyes. "My mom's just stubborn sometimes."

Annie wasn't so sure Claudia could be persuaded about anything. Not even her own daughter could convince her to change her mind. After Noah hugged Lainey one more time and said goodbye, he and Annie walked back out to his vehicle.

She gave him a withered glance as they both buckled in. "That went well, didn't it?"

"You're not ready to give up, are you?"

Annie shook her head. Change never happened when people gave up. "We'll figure something out." She returned his smile. Annie didn't know what possessed her, but she reached out and gripped Noah's hand. "I guess we're lost in the woods again, and we have to find the way out. We've got this."

Noah turned his hand over, so he was holding hers now. He nodded, his gaze locked on hers. "Yeah, Annie Taylor. We've got this."

He gave her hand a gentle squeeze before releasing her so he could start the Jeep.

The way he looked at her from the driver's seat told her he

was feeling the same hope she was, that they would figure out a way to fix this current problem, with or without Claudia's cooperation.

Annie read even more in his tender gaze. She saw the hope that together they would eventually figure everything out.

Right now, that was all the reassurance she needed.

CHAPTER 8

Crestpoint Beach's Gift Emporium was a chaotic display of town pride, showcasing the town's name on nearly every piece of merchandise in the store. The building was hardly bigger than a cottage, but its walls were filled with shelves boasting all sorts of souvenirs, ranging from painted seashells to shark's teeth to decorative mugs.

When Noah entered the shop, he had to wind through racks full of colorful T-shirts emblazoned with "Crestpoint Beach" or some other graphic art relating to the town. He'd come there to shop for something funky and fun to put in Lainey's room before it was his week with her again, but the main reason he chose the Emporium was because Annie's sister, Hannah, was working today and he was in need of a little advice.

He spotted Hannah's blonde hair behind the counter where she was helping a family of tourists buy a bunch of towels and flip-flops for a day at the beach. Noah busied himself near a display of mood rings and woven bracelets, waiting for her to wrap up with her customers.

He heard the digital doorbell sound as the family exited the store. When he turned around, Hannah was already making a beeline for him, a broad smile on her face.

"Hey, Noah!" She glanced at the gaudy mood ring he was holding in his palm, then gave him an intrigued look. "Shopping for anyone I know?"

"Ah, no." He shook his head, chuckling as he put the ring back in its display. "Actually, I was hoping to find something interesting for Lainey."

"Cool. What kind of stuff is she into these days?"

Noah shrugged, trying to recall Annie's easy assessment of his daughter's style and interests. "Got anything alternative or avant-garde?"

Hannah laughed. "Avant-garde? Well, we do have our lovely 'Oysters Playing Poker' gift collection over there."

"I don't think so," Noah said, grinning along with her. "Lainey does like dolphins, though. Preferably not the poker-playing variety."

"Right," Hannah's blue eyes gleamed bright with humor. "Follow me."

Being around Annie and her younger sister had always been easy for him, and the Taylor house had felt like something of a second home to him growing up. He'd missed that closeness after Annie left for college. Guilt over how he'd hurt her had kept Noah away from Hannah and Frank Taylor for years. Maybe he was punishing himself by shutting them out of his life the same way he had shut Annie out of his.

Either way, it was water over the dam now. All he could do was be grateful for the second chance he felt he might have again with Annie. If that second chance meant they would only stay friends, he'd find a way to be satisfied with that, but he would only be lying to himself if he tried to pretend he wasn't hoping for something more. His feelings for her were only getting stronger and more complicated each time they saw each other.

"Okay, here we are," Hannah announced, sweeping her hand out like she was a hostess on a game show. "Behold, the Gift Emporium's latest in dolphin-inspired finery."

"Impressive," Noah teased, taking in the tackiness. "I didn't even realize dolphin neckties were a thing."

Hannah giggled. "Oh, yeah. And check this out. Dolphin salt-and-pepper shakers. Or maybe Lainey would prefer this hat shaped like a dolphin?"

Noah chuckled as she modeled the silly hat for him. Something else caught his eye in the display. He reached for what looked like a dark snow globe. "What's this one?"

"Oh, that's actually pretty neat."

Hannah took it out of his hands and flipped on a switch in the wooden base. The dark globe illuminated with a pair of holographic dolphins captured in mid-leap coming out of a wave. It was exactly the kind of thing Lainey would love.

"Sold," he said.

Hannah grinned. "Awesome. Gift box?"

"Sure. Thanks."

"No problem." Hannah gestured for him to come with her to the counter. "So, Annie tells me you two are spending time together again. That's...interesting."

Noah pulled out his wallet and thumbed through his cash, if only to dodge her probing look. "We're just trying to work out some way to help the kids have their prom. Annie's been a lot of help, Plus, she's had some great ideas."

"That's Annie for you," Hannah agreed. "She's amazing, isn't she? You couldn't ask for a better partner."

Noah glanced up and placed his money on the counter,

uncertain if she was speaking about her sister as his partner on the school situation, or something else. He knew better than to ask. Hannah had never made a secret of her hopes for Annie's and his future together. And she was right about Annie being a great partner.

Having her support a couple of days ago with Claudia only made Noah respect Annie all the more. She had always been strong, courageous, and compassionate, even as a girl. As a woman now, she was a marvel in his eyes. The fact that she handled meeting both Lainey and Claudia with equal confidence and grace had blown him away.

When they'd gone back to his Jeep and she reached for his hand, it had taken all of his self-control not to draw her closer and kiss her the way he'd wanted to do that first time at the beach house. He didn't think a kiss in his ex-wife's driveway was a good idea, nor was he certain Annie wouldn't pull away from him the way she had before.

There was a lot he wasn't certain about when it came to Annie, other than his growing feelings for her and the ones he'd never lost in the first place.

"How's she doing, Hannah? I mean, after what happened to Derek."

Hannah lifted her shoulder as she placed Lainey's gift in a small box, a soft look coming into her eyes. "She's doing all right, I think. She still has moments when she struggles. Before she moved into the beach house, I'd hear her in her bedroom at Dad's house crying in the middle of the night. She's broken down a couple other times too, once when we were watching TV together, and again when she was fixing dinner. She didn't know I saw her, and I hurried out of the kitchen to let her have her privacy."

Noah frowned, a tight feeling in his chest when he thought

back on what Annie had confided in him about Derek's accident and her unwarranted guilt over it. He hated to think of her in the kind of pain Hannah had described. She was still grieving and here he was, contemplating the next time he might have the chance to hold her hand again or kiss her.

Hannah stared at him, her head tilted to the side. "The only times she seems really happy is when she's with you, or when she's talking about you."

He let go of the breath that had gotten jammed in his chest. "Really?"

Hannah nodded. "So, don't hurt her again, Noah. Please?"

"I don't intend to," he said, meaning it with everything he was worth. "I never wanted to hurt her at all."

"But you did," she reminded him. "Now, you have the opportunity to fix your mistake and make my sister really happy, so it might be a good idea for you to take that chance before it passes you by."

"What do you suggest?"

"That's not for me to say." Smiling encouragingly, she pushed the paper bag containing his purchase across the counter to him. "What I can tell you is that Annie's working at the beach house right now. Maybe by the time you get there, you'll think of a few ideas."

He ran his hand over his head and blew out a sigh before grabbing Lainey's gift. "Thanks, Hannah. For the shopping help and the advice."

Her voice rang out behind him as he headed for the exit. "Good luck, Noah!"

He made the short drive and parked on the sand-dusted street at the back of the house.

As he walked around to the veranda facing the water, he noticed that since the last time he was there, Annie had weeded out the flower beds that ran around the perimeter of the Victorian. Now they burst with explosions of pink perennials and beach roses, making the house's freshly painted sky-blue exterior pop. The white gingerbread trim gleamed, and pots overflowing with more bright blooms welcomed him as he walked up the short steps of the porch to the front door.

He had to knock four times before he heard Annie call out in reply. "I'll be right there!"

A few moments later, the door was pulled open, revealing Annie in a paint-spattered purple tank top and cut-offs. Her hair was gathered at her nape in a messy bun, showing off the light glow of her face as the late afternoon sunlight reflected in from the beach.

"Oh, hey! What are you doing here?" Annie asked him, tilting her head curiously.

"I was in town picking up something for Lainey, and uh… you've got some paint…" He pointed to her cheek with a light chuckle. A smear of light gray paint tracked from the right side of her nose to her jaw.

Annie rubbed the backs of her hands against both sides of her face and laughed. "I've been upstairs on the third floor painting the bedroom. I don't think I've checked a mirror all day."

"No need," he said. "You look beautiful—with paint or without."

Now a faint blush filled her face, too. Leaning against the door frame while he stood on the veranda, she crossed her arms. "So, what prompted you to stop by? Has anything else happened with Claudia or the board?"

"No, nothing's changed. I just thought I'd check in and see how you're doing on the house."

"You want to come in?" She stepped aside and he walked past her into the living area. "Wow, you've been busy."

"Yeah, I have. What do you think?"

He nodded, noting the handful of new pieces she'd added and the collection of framed coastal-themed photographs and art on the walls. In addition to looking like something out of a magazine, the big house was also beginning to look like a home.

"It's amazing, Annie." He looked at her, realizing what he really wanted to say was that she was amazing.

"Thanks." She hooked her thumb over her shoulder. "I've got a tray full of poured paint waiting upstairs that I shouldn't let dry out. Do you mind if we talk up there?"

"Sure, no problem. Need any help?"

"Are you serious?" She raised her brows, eyeing the white button-down and light khakis he'd worn all day at the school. "You might get messy."

He shrugged. "Tell me what you need me to do."

She smiled. "All right, then."

They jogged up the steps to the third floor, which opened up into one large living space with a prime view of the beach and water beyond. The room was empty, except for the drop cloths spread out on the floor and Annie's painting supplies. She'd already rolled light gray paint on two of the walls, but had apparently only gotten halfway through the third when he interrupted her work.

"Would you rather roll, or paint baseboards?" she asked him as they stood together inside the room.

He pointed to the long-handled roller. "I'll finish the walls. My painting skills are too rusty for precision work like baseboards and edging."

"Deal," she said. "My arms were getting tired, anyway."

Noah rolled up his sleeves and got right to work where she'd left off. Anne poured some creamy white paint into a small container, then grabbed a couple of different-sized brushes and hunkered down on the floor to begin on the baseboards.

"Has Lainey's desk come in yet?" she asked.

"Yeah, everything arrived yesterday. I can't wait for her to see it when she's back with me next week." He settled into a rhythm with the roller as he spoke, spreading the soothing, fog-gray paint over the wall. "I added a small file cabinet and a matching bookcase to the order. Lainey's a big reader."

"Just like her dad, huh?"

He chuckled. "She's like me in a lot of ways. Unfortunately, I think that's why Claudia struggles with her sometimes. Lainey reminds her too much of me."

Annie made an acknowledging noise, but went quiet for a few moments. "I have to admit, I was surprised to hear you married Claudia Harrow. She was part of the rich kids' clique and hung out with all the popular students. I didn't even realize you knew her. She and her friends acted as if we didn't exist."

Noah exhaled a sigh. "There was a reason for that."

"There was?" Annie set down her paintbrush and gave him her full attention. "Spill it, Davis."

He chuckled as he put another up-and-down column of paint on the wall, then lowered the roller into the tray at his feet. He faced Annie's inquisitive stare. "I tutored Claudia in geometry and science our entire senior year."

"What?" Annie gaped. "How did I not know this?"

"She made me promise not to tell anyone."

"But she was our class valedictorian. She got straight As all through school and made it look easy."

Noah nodded. "In reality, she had to work incredibly hard for those grades. By senior year, the pressure was starting to be too much. Her grades were slipping in both classes, and Claudia had the kind of parents where failure was not an option. So, she hired me as her private tutor—on the condition that no one knew about the arrangement."

Annie's gaze softened on him. "And you came to her rescue, because that's who you are, Noah Davis."

He shrugged, warmed by her praise. "I don't like to see anyone struggle with learning. Tutoring Claudia and seeing her improve her grades because of my help really solidified my decision to go into teaching. So, I benefited from it, too."

"Is that how you and Claudia ended up getting married so soon after graduation?"

He knew what she was really asking. Why had he gotten together with someone else so quickly after she had gone away to college? He hadn't expected to talk about his past with Annie today, but he figured now was as good a time as any to let this skeleton out of his closet.

"That summer after graduation, Claudia was having problems at home. She started spending more time with me to avoid being around her parents. I wasn't looking to start dating, but eventually one thing led to another and..." He released a heavy sigh. "When she told me she was pregnant, there was only thing for me to do."

"You married her."

He nodded. "We had a small ceremony at her family's church the next month. Claudia worked full-time at her family's boutique in town, and I worked during the day and took night classes at the community college to get my teaching certificate."

Annie's reaction wasn't judgmental, as he'd feared it might

be. Instead, she looked at him in sympathy and understanding. "If Claudia was already having issues at home, what did her family think about your situation?"

"Her parents were furious with both of us. My mom wasn't happy about it, either, but she supported our decision to get married. Who knows what my father might've thought if he hadn't abandoned my mom and me and never looked back. All I knew was, I wanted to be a better father to my kid than he was to me."

"And you are," Annie said. "You're amazing with Lainey. It's obvious she adores you."

"Thanks for saying that." He frowned, shaking his head. "I know you remember how hard I took it when my parents divorced. You were the one who got me through it, after all. One thing I always told myself was that I'd never put a child of mine through that kind of pain. Yet that's exactly what I did with Lainey."

Annie stood up and walked over to him. "You did the best you could, Noah. I have no doubt about that. Being divorced isn't a failure. It's how you handle it yourself and for the people involved that really counts. You're not your father, so don't ever think you are."

As he listened, he couldn't help the feeling of gratitude that built inside him. Annie's friendship had been a gift he'd sorely missed over the years. "You always did know just what I needed to hear, even when we were kids."

"I'm just telling you the truth. Isn't that what friends do for each other?"

"Yeah," he said, imagining how different his life would have been if Annie had stayed in Crestpoint Beach after high school. In a flash of pure selfishness, he wished she had. He wished for a lot of things where Annie was concerned. Then, and now.

She hooked a loose strand of hair behind her ear, and the motion drew his gaze to her pretty blue eyes...and to her mouth as she nervously sank her teeth into her lower lip. She wiped at the cheek that still had the paint smudge on it. "I should go clean the paint off my face."

"Sure. Okay." Noah cleared his throat. "My roller's dry, too. You didn't invite me in to bend your ear all afternoon, right? I came in to work."

Before he was tempted to do or say something reckless, he replenished the paint in his tray and went back to smoothing it onto the wall.

Annie disappeared for several minutes, a floorboard creaking somewhere in the hallway as she walked over it and then back again. When she returned, the paint on her cheek was scrubbed away and there was a new sense of resolve in her eyes.

"I may have to hire you to help me finish the rest of the rooms, Noah. You're a lot faster than I am."

Her humor eased the tension that had built between them before she left the room. He sent her a smile. "I'll be happy to lend a hand with whatever you need. All you have to do is call and put me to work."

She laughed. "You may regret offering. Hannah's been trying to convince me that we should convert the house into a bed-and-breakfast in time for the heavy tourist season. I have to admit, I've been giving it some thought, too."

"No kidding? I think it's a great idea."

"You do?"

"Sure. The house is certainly big enough for multiple

guests, plus you couldn't ask for a better location. You'd probably be booked solid most of the year."

She made a contemplative sound in the back of her throat as she continued painting the baseboards. "If we did finish fixing it up in time, how would we get the word out in time to catch this year's tourist traffic? It would only be a few months away."

"Well, you see, there's this thing called the internet." A small projectile hit the side of his head. The small wad of blue masking tape bounced off and landed on the drop cloth at his feet. He chuckled, looking Annie's way. "All joking aside, I can think of a dozen different ways for you to promote this place when you're ready."

"*If* we do it," she said, hedging now.

"Right. If you do it."

They went back to working, filling the time with light conversations about some of the people they both knew in school, about Lainey and her eclectic interests, and life in general.

After Noah had finished rolling the first coat of paint and then the second, Annie put the final touches on the room's baseboards.

"Great teamwork," she said, high-fiving him in the first-floor living area as he prepared to leave the house.

"The best," he replied. "I meant what I said, Annie. Call me if you need any other help."

She tilted her head, a smile curving her lips. "I will."

He hesitated, reluctant to leave. Aside from dropping the bomb on her about his marriage with Claudia and the circumstances of Lainey's birth, and then narrowly resisting his attraction to Annie in the bedroom, the time they'd spent together had been great. He wasn't ready for it to end.

"Do you have any dinner plans tonight?"

Her eyes went a little wider. "Um, usually I have dinner with my dad and Hannah."

"Oh, sure. Of course."

"But I don't have to. Why? Do you have something in mind?"

"I thought maybe we could grab a bite somewhere." He shrugged, trying to play it casual. He was so rusty at this kind of thing, he probably just looked awkward. He felt awkward, like a geeky teen all over again.

Annie frowned, tilting her head. "You mean, like a date?"

"No." The denial burst out of him.

It was a defensive reflex more than anything else, because he actually had meant he wanted to take her out for a date. Unless she wasn't ready for that. Based on the shocked, uncertain look on her face now, he prepared himself for a flat rejection.

He shoved his hands into his pockets. "You've been so great with Lainey and with jumping in to help me look for solutions to the cuts at school, I'd like to do something nice for you as a thank you."

"Oh," she said, her shoulders relaxing. "I see. All right."

"Is that a yes?"

She nodded. "Sure. Why not?"

He let go of the breath he didn't realize he was holding. "Great. I'll pick you up around seven?"

"Okay. Where should we go?"

"You leave that to me. I think I remember all of the places you used to enjoy."

Her brows lifted. "A surprise, then."

"I promise I won't disappoint you," he said, instantly

recalling how terribly he had done just that the night of their prom some seventeen years ago.

She must have been thinking about it, too. The smile that had been playing along the edges of her mouth faded a little as she watched him step out the door.

"Thanks again for your help today, Noah. I'll see you at seven. For our non-date."

"Yeah. See you then, Annie."

He mentally kicked himself as he raised his hand and waved goodbye while she stood behind him on the veranda in the orange glow of the sunset.

CHAPTER 9

Annie didn't remember the last time she'd spent so long getting ready. She hadn't gone to dinner with a man other than Derek in forever, and she hardly knew what to do with herself or what to expect. However, it comforted her to know it was Noah who was coming to get her, and that technically, it wasn't a date.

Even though it felt like a date.

Drawing in a deep breath, Annie checked her reflection one more time in the mirror of her second-floor bedroom's adjoining bathroom. Despite the beach house being too big for just her alone, it was still nice to be there and to have some privacy.

Her sleep had steadily improved, thanks to the constant roar of the surf outside. She still had her moments of sorrow now and then, those awful times when the tears just sprang up from nowhere when something unexpected would remind her of Derek and the guilt that continued to cling to her over the day of his death.

But even that was slowly improving.

Being around her family helped immensely, and so did spending time with Noah.

Annie hoped she hadn't gone overboard on getting ready. He'd said their dinner wasn't intended as a date, but that didn't mean she shouldn't try to look nice. Acceptable dinner attire around Crestpoint Beach ranged from fresh-off-the-beach casual to full-on glam, so she had opted for something in the middle.

She'd finally settled on a sleeveless, black skater dress with a fitted bodice and an A-line skirt that hit just above her knee, paired with black flats that could pass for dressed-up or dressed-down. Her hair was curled into loose, beachy waves that broke around her shoulders, and she'd gone light on her makeup—just some mascara and dusky-rose lip color. Since her face seemed to provide its own blush when she was near Noah, the only thing she'd put on her cheeks was some moisturizer.

When Annie heard a knock on the front door of the beach house, her heart leaped into her throat, coaxing her to hurry down the wooden staircase and cross the floor to the foyer. She pulled the door open to reveal Noah in a charcoal-gray blazer, a white button-down, and black pants. His rich brown hair lifted in the breeze blowing in from the water, giving him a tousled look that only made him look even more handsome. Even against the darkness of night behind him, he seemed to glow as he looked at her.

"Hi," Annie greeted him, her cheeks already warming as she watched his eyes sweep up and down, drinking her in.

"You look incredible, Annie."

"You clean up pretty well, too," she said, returning his smile.

He stepped back to let her out of the house. "Are you ready to go?"

She nodded, retrieving her small black purse off the accent table near the door on her way out. She locked up, then turned to find Noah extending his arm out to help her down the porch steps and onto the sand below.

"Just a second," she said, holding on to him a little tighter as she reached down and took off her flats to make the short walk to where he'd parked his Jeep.

Her heart rate quickened the longer she touched him, but she couldn't seem to let go of his muscled arm until they reached his vehicle and he'd escorted her to the passenger side. He waited while she got situated in her seat, then he carefully closed the door for her and jogged around to his side.

"I hope I'm not overdressed for wherever we're going."

He fastened his seatbelt, then glanced at her as he started the engine, his eyes gleaming in the lights of the dashboard. "You're perfect. And if that was a cagey way of persuading me to ruin the surprise, it won't work."

She laughed. "You know me too well. I can't put anything past you."

"You'll at least have to try a little harder than that," he teased, pulling out onto the road to head along the beach. Noah turned his attention back to the road, streetlights illuminating the asphalt through the darkness.

His surprises were always better than hers. She had no willpower, especially when he'd turn on the charm to get her to cave and give him easy clues to guess what she was trying to hide. She couldn't help it, unable to deny herself the pleasure of his awed face whenever she revealed her surprise, which was usually a gift she thought he'd like, or something for them to share together.

"It's good to know you're still as stubborn as ever," she remarked, feeling more comfortable with him by the minute. He made it so easy to slide back into their old friendship, even after seventeen years. Being with him felt as easy as coming home.

He chuckled, navigating the Jeep toward the town pier. "All right, I'll give you a clue. We're almost there."

Annie leaned forward to look out the windshield, her breath catching in genuine surprise.

"The Sunset Grill? As I recall, it used to be you couldn't get near the door without a reservation at least a week in advance."

"You still can't," Noah replied. "I have a few connections. Surprised?"

She grinned. "Okay, you got me. Yes, I'm totally surprised."

"Good."

He swung up to the valet, and in moments the attendant had whisked the Jeep away. Noah held out his arm to her again, and they walked onto the wooden pier that led to the elegant restaurant perched atop the water at the end.

Sunset Grill was the most popular eatery in town. With large dining room windows overlooking the gulf and golden string lights lining the exterior with its wide deck and romantic outdoor seating, the Grill was Crestpoint Beach's premier date-night destination. Which made it an interesting choice for her non-date with Noah.

Annie tried to ignore the heat from his hand at the small of her back as they entered the restaurant and approached the hostess stand. Couples crowded the entryway, waiting on foot and seated on the narrow benches just inside the door. The young brunette handling reservations and table assignments smiled when she spotted Noah.

"Good evening, Mr. Davis. Ma'am." She nodded politely at Annie before collecting a pair of menus from the stand and stepping around to join them. "We have your table ready for you. Right this way."

"Thank you, Natalie."

Annie glanced at Noah as they weaved their way through the packed dining room to a vacant table for two at the windows. His handsome profile gave away nothing as they approached their table and took their seats. A small candle danced in a hurricane lamp between them in front of the window, its golden reflection gleaming.

Natalie handed Annie one of the brass-edged, black leatherbound menus before giving the second one to Noah. "Michael will be your server tonight," she announced. "He'll be right with you."

Noah murmured his thanks as the hostess departed. His gaze held Annie's. "Is this table all right with you?"

"Are you kidding? It's amazing." She leaned forward and lowered her voice to a whisper. "How on earth did you manage this—with no notice, besides?"

"Natalie was a student of mine. Her parents own this place now. You might remember her father, Ed Sanchez. We went to school with him."

Annie nodded. "Yes, I remember. You guys did that lab project together that took first prize in the science fair our freshman year. You called in a favor for me?"

He shrugged as if he did this kind of thing every day. "I wanted to do something special for you. I hope you're pleased."

"Noah, we could leave right now and I'd still be totally impressed. Thank you for doing this."

"You're welcome, Annie. He smiled, but there was a note of seriousness in the way he looked at her from across the table as they settled in and opened their menus.

After deciding to each have a glass of wine and share an appetizer of seared scallops, Annie ordered the chef's special grilled tuna, and Noah opted for the surf and turf. They went right back to talking, a sense of comfort and ease settling over them as they caught up on things going on in Crestpoint Beach and some of the other areas that had been familiar to them when they were growing up. Annie couldn't remember the last time she smiled and laughed so much. Noah made it easy for her to relax and just have fun, something he'd always had a knack for when it came to her.

He glanced up at her as he sliced off a bite of his steak. "Speaking of places we used to know, our tree is still there on the playground at the elementary school."

"Is it?" Annie took a sip of her wine, feeling her face warm at the reminder. She didn't have to ask him to elaborate on the old oak's significance to them. She still remembered that moment in vivid detail. Noah had kissed her under that tree when they were in fifth grade. He tasted like strawberries because their class had just been rewarded with lollipops for being quiet during lunch, while the other classes were loud. The kiss only lasted a few seconds, but she remembered it feeling like the most magical moment she had ever experienced.

It had been the moment her ten-year-old heart fell head over heels in love with Noah Davis. She had cherished that innocent peck on the lips every day since, carrying its memory close even now.

Even after Noah had broken that same tender heart without explanation years later.

She set her glass down and dabbed her napkin at the edges of her mouth, hoping her dimmed mood didn't show. "That tree must be close to a hundred years old. I'm glad to hear it's still standing."

"Well, it's had some close shaves, but there's a lot of love for it in town. A few years ago, I tasked the kids in my science club with studying oak tree parasites and diseases, and we wrote up a care plan for the tree and presented it to the town. Now, there's at least a dozen young adults who are invested in preserving it, too."

Annie stared at him, finding it impossible to not be moved by the depth of his involvement, not just with his students, but with the town and its future. "That was a really thoughtful thing to do."

He held his glass in one hand as he gazed at her. "I have to admit, I've got ulterior motives when it comes to preserving that particular piece of history. If I have my way, that old tree will be standing long after I'm gone."

Annie didn't know what to say, nor could she hold his meaningful stare. She went back to her dinner, abruptly changing the subject to less emotion-laden topics.

Noah listened politely and asked thoughtful questions as she told him about her design plans for various rooms in the beach house, and about some of the most challenging projects she had undertaken throughout her career. She told him about a few of the design awards she'd won, and about the company she had been building with Derek before that part of her life had come crashing down around her.

"It sounds like things really took off for you in Dallas," he remarked, studying her with a proud, contemplative expression. "I had no doubts that you were going to shine, Annie."

His praise meant the world to her, not just because he knew how big her dreams had been back then, but because Noah had been her best friend.

Her everything, if she was being honest with herself.

Once dinner came to a close and they strode out of the restaurant, Noah's fingers brushed her arm to stop her from walking ahead. He nodded toward the beach on the other side of the pier, where the pale sand glowed and the moonlight rippled off the surface of the dark water.

"It's warm tonight. Want to take a walk?" Noah asked her.

"Sure."

They walked down the sidewalk to one of the wood-plank steps leading down onto the beach. At the bottom of it, Annie reached out to take Noah's arm as she slipped her shoes off. He took his off too, stuffing his socks inside.

"I'll carry those for you," he offered, taking her flats in the same hand as his own shoes as he led her onto the cool sand. The tide was going out, leaving a broad stretch of beach between the dunes and the white-capped waves lapping at the shore. The steady roll and crash of the surf was the rhythm of her childhood, and of more than a few nights that she and Noah had strolled along this same stretch of beach as teens.

Annie drew in a deep breath through her nose to try to calm her heart, which was rapidly thumping in her chest to feel the warmth of Noah's body as he walked at her side. If they were still lovestruck teenagers, he would've already linked his fingers through hers. Instead, he carried their shoes in the hand opposite her, and had his free hand tucked into the front pocket of his slacks.

Annie folded her arms in front of her, feeling all too aware of the fact that they were no longer a couple. Seventeen years put a lot of space and life lived between them, even if there were times when it seemed to her heart as though time had stood still.

"Are you cold?" Noah asked, pausing. "Why don't you take my jacket?"

Before she could assure him she was fine, he set their shoes down then shrugged out of the black sport coat and wrapped it around her shoulders. It was still warm from his body heat. That warmth, and the amazing scent of him, wreathed her senses as they slowly continued along the moonlit beach.

After they'd gone a few yards in companionable silence, he said, "I've been thinking some more about fundraising ideas. I'm sure I can convince my science club kids to pitch in on a car wash weekend or two. We could also get the kids involved with setting up donation jars at some of the local businesses."

Annie nodded, picturing the possibilities. "Those are great ideas. I was thinking that maybe we could do a big sale right at the school gymnasium and have it decorated with some of the prom's theme elements to remind people of what their contributions are supporting. We could even have the juniors and seniors provide photos of themselves and write a few lines about what prom and some of the cut programs mean to them. We could display the photos and notes in poster form for the community members to read as they browse the sale."

Noah's handsome face lit up with enthusiasm. "Those are fantastic ideas. I'll work on getting on the gym. What do you think we could sell at this fundraiser?"

"Anything and everything. We could add a shoe drive, and maybe a raffle of some kind to raise extra money. We could make it a true community effort."

"I like it," he said, pausing to turn toward her. His warm gaze was like a caress on her face. Unspoken thoughts seemed to fill his eyes as he studied her in a way that made her heart beat with anticipation. "I can't thank you enough for pitching in like this, Annie. It means a lot to me. You…mean a lot to me."

He lifted his free hand to her cheek, gently sweeping aside a tendril of her hair that caught on the breeze off the water. As he hooked the strand behind her ear, his touch lingered against her face. Annie breathed in through her parted lips, knowing she should step away from that sweet caress, but she couldn't.

Standing on the beach under the moonlight with him felt so familiar and comforting. It felt so right, like truly coming home again.

Except nothing was the same now. They were different people. Their lives had traveled down very different paths. And there was still one big unanswered question left hanging between them.

Annie gazed up at him, awash in a confusing mix of hope and regret. "Noah, why didn't you show up that night? I waited for you for hours. I called you multiple times, but you never answered. Why?"

He frowned and slowly shook his head, exhaling a heavy breath. His hand fell away from her cheek. "Annie, I am so, so sorry for the way I handled that. The truth is, I got scared. Things were moving so fast between us that year—"

"Moving so fast? You were my best friend for years. I thought we were in love."

"We were," he agreed quietly. "And you had your whole life ahead of you, a life that was bigger than Crestpoint Beach. You had dreams, Annie. You had a scholarship from the

University of Texas and you were considering turning it down."

Hurt cracked open in her chest. "I didn't care where I went to college. I could've just as easily gone to school somewhere closer to home."

"If you had, none of those things you told me about at dinner tonight would've happened. There wouldn't have been the big design firm in Dallas, or the career awards, or the big projects that still light up your whole face when you talk about them. You wouldn't have had your time with Derek, either."

She couldn't deny any of those facts. Nor could she regret a moment of her career or her short marriage to Derek. In her heart, she also knew that if she had stayed, Noah wouldn't have Lainey, and his daughter was something he would never regret too.

None of that lessened the hurt of the way things had ended with Noah. She had carried the confusion from that night for the past seventeen years.

"You didn't want me to stay here, so you stood me up?" She folded her arms in front of her, feeling no anger toward him, only bewilderment and sadness. "You ignored my calls that whole night. Then, in school the next week, you avoided me. Every time you saw me coming, you turned the other way. I thought I had done something wrong."

"Annie...no." He sounded nearly as pained as she felt. Remorse filled his expression. "You didn't do anything wrong. It was me. I was a stupid kid. I didn't know how else to handle everything I was feeling. I should have talked to you, but I didn't know if I would've been strong enough to tell you to go. I wasn't sure you'd listen, even if I had been able to say the words."

She knew he was right. She had adored him so much, she would have done anything to stay with him. There was nothing she wouldn't have sacrificed if it meant being with Noah.

That didn't make his actions hurt any less.

"Annie," he said, resting his hand against her shoulder. "I've owed you an explanation—and my apology—for a very long time. Please know that I am sorry for hurting you. Losing your friendship was the hardest thing I've ever gone through."

She looked up at him, hearing the sincerity in his voice. She could see it in his eyes.

"Can you forgive me? Now that you know, can you find it in your heart to let me try to win back your trust?" He gave her an uncertain smile. "Can we still be friends?"

Friends. She hadn't come home expecting to reconnect with him romantically. She hadn't been ready to as much as consider opening her heart back up to falling in love, yet for some reason his question brought a pang of disappointment.

She'd never imagined she would have a second chance with Noah, but that's what the past couple of weeks had felt like to her. It felt like more than just a rekindling of their friendship, but maybe she was reading more into it than was there. Maybe some unresolved, wounded part of her was only wishing they could go back to what they'd had before their crushing breakup.

She managed to smile through her complicated tangle of emotions as she gazed up at him. "You'll always be my friend, Noah."

She meant it. Their bond had been formed so long ago, it was impossible to imagine being in Crestpoint Beach and not having him in her life in some way. Even during her years in

Dallas, when she missed being home those thoughts always included Noah.

Relief flooded his expression. "Thank you. Thank you for coming with me tonight, too. I'm glad we had this chance to talk."

"I am too." She shrugged out of his jacket and draped it over her arm in front of her. "It's getting late. I should probably get home soon."

"Yeah. Okay, sure."

They trudged back up the sand to the restaurant valet, then made the drive back to the beach house in silence. He parked on the street and walked her around to the porch, waiting beside her as she unlocked the door.

She turned to face him, the door open at her back. "Thank you for dinner, Noah."

"Anytime. Thank you for giving me another chance." He stared at her for a moment, his eyes drifting to her lips. "I should go now."

"Yes," she said, terrified that she might do something embarrassing like close the distance and kiss him the way she longed to do. "Well, goodnight, then."

"Goodnight, Annie."

She stepped inside the house and slowly closed the door, leaving him standing on the veranda in the dim yellow glow of the porch light.

It wasn't until she heard his footsteps retreating that she sagged back against the door and let out a broken sigh.

CHAPTER 10

*L*ater that week, Noah dropped by Annie's house to update her on the fundraising tasks he'd taken on following the brainstorming session they'd had after dinner at Sunset Grill.

As he walked up to the veranda and knocked on the door, the scents of warm vanilla, cinnamon, and butter greeted his nose. Annie appeared a few moments later, dressed in shorts and a faded Crestpoint High marching band T-shirt. Over the top of it, she wore a pink-and-white striped apron that was dusted with flour.

"Hey, your timing is perfect," she said, her smile putting him instantly at ease. "I was just about to take a tray of peanut butter cookies out of the oven. You can help me with the next batch."

"Can I sample while I work?"

She laughed. "I guess that's a fair exchange. Come on in."

Noah had been anxious about seeing her again. Their dinner a few nights ago had been amazing until she had asked him to explain why he'd hurt her the way he had at their prom. She'd deserved to know long before now, and he could only be grateful that she'd been willing to forgive him at all. The fact that she was so accepting of his faults and failures only made him care even more deeply for her.

As if that was even possible. He truly had loved her when they were in school. A part of him had stayed in love with her long after she had moved away to Texas to chase her dreams. Now that she was back, it was as though all of the feelings he felt were dormant and buried in the years she was gone were now blooming back to life, even stronger than before.

That wasn't good, especially when he was aware of how she still grieved for her husband. He didn't want to rush her into anything she wasn't ready for, or pressure her to reciprocate on the feelings he had to combat every time she was near him.

"I've got some good news," he told her as he followed her into the kitchen and washed his hands at the sink. "The car wash is on as we speak, and I was actually able to secure two locations. One group of kids and some parent chaperones have set up in the grocery store parking lot, and the other group will be stationed on the opposite side of town next to the park."

"That's awesome," Annie said, moving in to wash up next to him. "We'll get people coming and going."

"Yep." He glanced at the island, which looked like a bakery startup. "How's it going here at Cookie Central?"

"You just missed Hannah. We've been baking since before dawn today. We've got twelve-dozen each chocolate chip and cinnamon raisin, plus ten-dozen sugar with sprinkles. I'm halfway through the peanut butter cookies now."

Noah smiled. "Something for everyone's tastes tonight at the sale. Good thinking."

"Go ahead and take one of the peanut butters while they're still warm. I know those are your favorite."

He ate it in two bites. "Tell me what you need me to do, boss."

She pulled a fresh apron out of a cabinet drawer and handed it to him. While he tied it on, she directed him to a bowl of light-brown cookie dough waiting on the island. "Roll a dozen for each of those sheets while I mix some more dough. The fork for pressing them is right here."

Annie had volunteered to host a bakery booth at the fundraiser at the school tonight. In addition to baked goods, there would be students and parents selling crafts, other foods, recreational classes, among scores of other things. The support they had received to put on the fundraiser was outstanding, and booth reservations to fill the school's gymnasium had gone quickly.

"Where's Lainey today?" Annie asked as she prepared more cookie dough in the mixer. "You should've brought her with you."

"It's Claudia's week." Noah began rolling his dough into balls and arranging them on the cookie sheets. "I tried to convince her to let Lainey participate in some of the fundraising activities, but Claudia isn't happy about us going over her head to try to save what she cut. She accused me of making her out to be the villain with Lainey."

"I'm sorry," Annie said, casting him a sympathetic look as she scooped peanut butter into her mixing bowl. "Based on what you told me about her situation growing up, I imagine Claudia's got a lot of insecurities."

"Yes, she does. I just wish she'd loosen the reins a little and stop punishing Lainey for her conflicts with me. She has this deep-seated need to be in control of everything, and that's not easy for Lainey. It wasn't easy for our marriage, either."

"Is that why you split up?"

He shrugged. "In the end, that was only one of a hundred reasons. I suppose the biggest one was that we weren't in love with each other."

"Oh." Annie went quiet, seeming to focus intently on her recipe.

"Claudia was a good mother," he added, feeling the need to fill the silence. "For the most part, she's a good mother now, too. Co-parenting isn't easy. Claudia manages to keep our schedules smooth for Lainey, and she does try to do what's best for her. She's just wound so tight. She's not always as patient or accepting as I wish she was, and she doesn't seem to know when to stand back and let Lainey learn or fail or grow."

"Those things are hard," Annie said, sifting some flour into the mixing bowl. "I should say, I can imagine they'd be hard for a parent to do."

Noah pressed the fork into the last cookie he'd formed on his tray and glanced at Annie. "Had you and Derek talked about having kids one day?"

She lifted her shoulder. "We talked about it. Having a family wasn't a priority for him."

"What about you? You used to talk all the time about wanting a family of your own. A girl and a boy."

Something flickered in her gaze before she glanced back down at the dough in her bowl. "That was a long time ago, Noah. Life takes us in different directions sometimes."

"Yeah, I guess it does."

She glanced past him at a few ingredients next to him. "Could you pass me the brown sugar, please?"

He nodded, wiping his hands on a damp cloth on the counter near the sink and then passing the bag of sugar to her. Their fingers brushed as she took it from him. Even that small touch sent a jolt through him, speeding his heart rate. He remembered how soft her cheek felt against his fingertips the other night on the beach, how warm her skin felt even now.

It was torture being around her sometimes because it only reminded him of how happy they had been once. There were so many "what ifs" between them now, countless agonizing "if onlys". Trying to keep their relationship casual and platonic would be the test of his lifetime, because all his heart wanted was Annie.

How often had he pictured his future with her at his side? He could still imagine it now, picturing her on the beach in a white dress with flowers in her hair and a ring on her finger—the one he would put there as they vowed in front of their family and friends to love, honor, and cherish each other for as long as they both should live.

Nothing had gone the way they planned. Divorce. Death. Miles of detours and years of lost time, but somehow their paths had eventually led them back to each other.

Annie drew in a deep breath, then released it. "Well, these cookies aren't going to bake themselves."

She grabbed a hand-mixer and placed the beaters into her bowl. She flicked the switch on the appliance, and in a burst of flour and raw egg, the dough splattered all over her and the kitchen. It even hit Noah standing about an arm's length away.

"Oops!" She gaped at him. "I swear, that was an accident."

She giggled into her hand at first, then bent over laughing as Noah pulled a string of egg yolk and clumps of dough out of his hair.

"Yeah? You think that's funny, do you?"

He flung some of the mess back at her. The sticky dough and egg clung to her chin.

"I can't believe you just did that," Annie gasped, staring at him in shock. A grin broke over her pretty, dough-spattered face. "Now, you're in for it, Davis."

Not a few seconds passed before they both started digging into the silver bowl to toss flour and smear egg all over each other. Annie backed up against Noah, attempting to duck her head away from him as he tried to throw brown sugar at her.

Noah automatically wrapped his arms around her, drawing her close to his chest as they shuffled across the floor, their laughter echoing throughout the kitchen.

"That's what you get," he teased her, caging her in his arms.

They were both laughing, both breathing hard before a calm settled over them, the cookie dough battle coming to an end as swiftly as it started.

Annie released the silver bowl, setting it on the counter in front of her. Noah still held her against him. It was an intimate embrace, one not meant for friends, and they both realized that. However, neither of them moved. Her body trembled as she slowly rested her hands over his for a moment. Then she stepped out of his embrace and turned to face him.

He was completely entranced. There was hardly any space between them. Annie stared up at him in silence, her blue eyes so deep he wanted to drown in them. Unable to hold himself back any longer, he brought his fingertips under her chin and leaned forward to press his lips to hers.

Annie's eyes fluttered closed and she leaned into his kiss, giving in as he pulled her closer. He cupped her face in his palms, his thumbs stroking across her heated cheeks. She tasted like vanilla and sugar, and she felt like heaven in his arms.

He might have kissed her forever, but the sudden trill of his phone on the counter broke them apart. He backed off at once, pivoting to grab the device. The ringtone told him who it was. "It's Lainey. I have to take this."

"Of course." She glanced down and spun away from him, though not before he saw the deep color in her cheeks.

Clearing his throat, he struggled to find his voice. "Hey, kiddo. What's up?"

A sob came over the line. "Mom and I had a fight."

Noah tensed. He had a bunch of questions, but first things first. "Are you okay?"

"Yes. I'm fine. But she's really mad." She sniffled. In the background were the sounds of vehicles and kids' voices.

"Lainey, where are you?"

"At the grocery store car wash with Mason." Another sniffle rasped into Noah's ear. "She told me I couldn't go to the fundraiser, but her only reason was because she didn't want me to."

"So, you went anyway?" He practically groaned.

"I called Mason and he picked me up. Mom's working at the boutique today, so why should I have to sit home and do nothing?"

"She's your mother, Lainey," he reminded her. "If she said she didn't want you to go, you need to respect that."

"Well, I did call her and tell her where I was," she hedged. "Now, she says I'm gonna be grounded when she gets home from work."

Noah ran his hand over his jaw and sent a frustrated glance at Annie. She was looking at him in concern, obviously picking up the gist of the conversation from his side alone.

"All right, I'm leaving right now," he told her. "I'm going to pick you up and bring you back to your mom's to wait for her."

"But, Dad—"

"I'm sorry, sweetheart. I can't help you with this one. You're going to have to face the music."

A fresh sob burst out of her. "Why won't she let me have any fun?"

"We can talk about that when I get there, okay? I'm not even ten minutes away."

"Fine," she sighed defeatedly, then murmured goodbye and they ended the call.

Noah slid the phone into his pocket and looked at Annie. "I have to go."

"I understand. Is Lainey all right?"

He nodded. "She's really stepped in it this time, though. She sneaked out with Mason to work the car wash against Claudia's wishes."

"Uh, oh."

"Yeah." Noah took off the apron and collected his keys. "I'm, uh, sorry I wasn't much help with the cookies."

He probably ought to apologize for the kiss he stole, too, but that was a conversation for another time.

"Don't worry about the cookies. Go get your daughter." Annie walked with him to the door. "Will I see you tonight at the fundraiser?"

"Wouldn't miss it for the world. Save me a cookie or two."

"Deal." She smiled as he stepped out to the veranda. "I'll see you there, Noah."

CHAPTER 11

Crestpoint High's gymnasium was filled with various booths selling all sorts of items and services.

A swell of chatter filled the space as teachers, students, parents, and community members moved from booth to booth to explore the many offerings provided to benefit the school's affected programs and events. Booths were made from tables, poster boards, and props, along with streamers, balloons, and glitter to make them attract the huge crowd packed into the gym that night. It had been a team effort, and the fundraiser was an obvious success not even an hour into the opening.

After dropping off numerous boxes of cookies to several of the baked goods stands situated around the event, Annie ventured through the crowd to find Hannah's booth, which displayed her hand-painted seashells and an assortment of her other crafts, ranging from wind chimes to jewelry to driftwood art.

"Do I get a family discount?" Annie jokingly asked as she moved to Hannah's side, seeing that she had already made a decent amount of money. Sellers took half of their profit and donated the other half to the cause, so Hannah would get some compensation for all of her hard work. Annie knew her sister spent a long time working on her seashells, whether she was collecting them, painting them, or crafting them into an artistic piece.

Hannah playfully tapped her forefinger against her chin in mock consideration. "For you, sis? Take anything you want, one-hundred percent off." Her humor dimmed as she stared at Annie. "You seem...off. What's wrong?"

Annie should've suspected that Hannah would quickly notice her tenseness. She hadn't been able to shake the thought of Noah and Lainey, her concern for both of them weighing on her since he'd left the house. Their unexpected kiss in the kitchen wasn't far from her mind, either.

As close as Annie was with her sister, it didn't seem right to share either of those developments before she saw Noah again.

"I'm fine," she said. "Just anxious about tonight's event."

That much was true, although. it didn't seem like she had much to worry about where the fundraiser was concerned. While she stood at Hannah's table, several customers came by to browse. Within minutes, two of them had chosen pieces of handcrafted art to buy.

Annie stepped aside to let Hannah handle the transactions, her gaze traveling over the throng of people who'd shown up for the sale. She was relieved to see it was so popular, but there was only one person she really wanted to see among the crowd.

As she watched more people file into the gym, she caught sight of Noah near the doors. He stepped inside with a dark-haired man around their age, both of them talking as if they were good friends. Noah spotted Annie across the large space and lifted his hand in acknowledgment before he and his companion headed for Hannah's booth.

Noah smiled as they approached, seeming casual now that he was in public among colleagues and the community, but Annie noted the subtle stress in his face.

"Hi," she said, giving him an understanding smile. "How are you doing?"

"All good for now," he replied, picking up her signal. "Looks like we have a hit on our hands here."

"Yes, it's been like this since the doors opened."

Noah gestured to the man at his side. "This is my friend Henry Park. He teaches algebra here at the high school. Henry, this is my friend Annie Collins and her sister, Hannah Taylor."

"Nice to meet you, Henry." Annie reached out and shook his hand. Hannah followed suit.

Henry gave them a warm smile, then glanced at the table full of handcrafts and funky art. "This is some cool stuff. Love the seashell wind chimes."

Hannah beamed. "Thank you! I made this group of them yesterday. I collected all of the shells for them from the beach right here in town."

Henry looked intrigued. "A true piece of local flavor, then. I've been looking for a housewarming gift for my buddy, Gabe, who just moved here recently from Denver. One of these would be a great choice, I think."

"Awesome," Hannah chirped. "What made your friend move here?"

"He came for work. He's a building contractor, looking to start a new business here in town." Henry picked up one of the chimes. "I'll take this one."

Annie glanced over at Noah with a smile as Hannah brought Henry to the other side of the table to cash him out. "At the rate this is going, Hannah's going to be out of product long before the night is over."

"Let's hope so. This sale was a great idea, Annie."

"How did it go at the car wash today?"

Noah's look said he knew she wasn't merely asking about the receipts. "Can you break away for a few minutes to talk?"

"Sure."

She motioned to Hannah that she would be back in a few minutes, then walked around the other side of the table to Noah. They began a slow stroll along the busy rows of booths filling the gymnasium.

"How's Lainey?" Annie asked, as they threaded their way through the clusters of people browsing and shopping.

Noah nodded. "She'll be fine. After I left your place, I picked her up at the car wash and dropped her back at her mom's to wait for Claudia to get home from work. Now, she's mad at both of us."

Annie winced. "I'm sorry."

He shook his head. "I may not always agree with Claudia's decisions or opinions, especially where Lainey's concerned, but that doesn't mean I'm going to condone Lainey disobeying her."

"Mother-daughter relationships can be complicated. Lainey's fortunate she has a mom who's there to care for her, even if they don't always see eye-to-eye," Annie pointed out."

"That's exactly what I told her today when I dropped her off," Noah said, his smile deepening as he glanced at her.

Annie flicked her gaze away from his, unable to look at him right now and not wonder what kind of parents they would have made together. She couldn't count how many times she'd imagined being married to him and having a family of their own. That kiss in her kitchen earlier today had brought a lot of those dreams and yearnings roaring back to life.

Was he feeling the same way? After telling her he wanted to be friends that night they'd walked the beach, she had gone home believing there was a chance that she and Noah might never be more than friends again. She'd made peace with that...mostly. Then he'd gone and kissed her, scrambling her emotions more than ever.

She wanted to talk about what happened and how he was feeling, but the crush of the people all around them made any meaningful conversation nearly impossible.

A group of teens rushed past them, one girl offering a giggled apology as she and her friends ran toward a specialty booth in the corner of the gym. Noah chuckled, then his brow furrowed when he saw where the kids were going.

"We have an old time photo booth in here? How on earth did you manage that?"

Annie laughed, her arm bumping against his as more kids jostled past them. "The Gift Emporium loaned theirs to us for the night. Hannah gets all the credit for that one."

"Remember how often we used to pose for those silly pictures?"

Annie smiled. "Of course, I remember. I still have our photo strips tucked away in a moving box I brought with me from Dallas."

He stared at her. "You saved them all this time?"

"Yes. It's not like I'd ever throw them away."

He made a noise of surprise in the back of his throat. As they neared the booth, his steps slowed to a halt. "What do you say? Should we add a few more to the collection?"

"Now?"

He grinned, gesturing around them. "Why not? You got somewhere else you need to be?"

She started to stammer out an excuse, but at that same moment the kids who had piled in ahead of them came scrambling out on peals of laughter to retrieve their photos as the strip plopped into the little basket outside the booth.

Noah took hold of her hand. "Come on, Annie. Seize the moment."

They ducked inside the cramped booth and Noah pulled her down onto the hard laminate bench with him. The seat was so narrow, she had to press up against his side for them to both fit. "These are smaller than I remember."

"We're not kid-size anymore," Noah reminded her with a chuckle as he set up the machine. He then looked at her with a curious look. "We should do a couple of silly ones for old times' sake."

"Okay," Annie replied with a nod. She turned toward the camera as it started to count down, racking her brain for one of her old poses. She stuck her tongue out and closed one eye as the flash went off, white filling her vision for a few seconds until it faded away. Next, she formed rabbit ears behind Noah's head, laughing when she felt him doing the same to her. "Smiles this time?"

Noah nodded, quickly moving to place his arm around her shoulder as the camera counted down again for their second photo. He leaned his head against hers as they smiled for the photo, the flash filling the booth once again. His arm remained around her shoulders, holding her close as they relaxed from posing.

Annie felt the pressure of the countdown. "What should we do now?"

They both turned their heads toward each other at the same time. Sitting as close as they were, his nose wasn't even an inch away from hers. They were close enough that she could feel his warm breath mingling with hers.

Her eyes drifted up to meet his, her body freezing as the camera counted down. She couldn't even think about forming a pose when his lips were so close to hers.

Close enough to kiss.

Suddenly, the flash went off, knocking her back to reality. With a nervous laugh, she drew back, putting a little distance between them on the bench. Noah's gaze stayed rooted on her, his handsome face solemn and unreadable.

"Noah, about what happened earlier at my house, in the kitchen..." she began hesitantly.

"Yeah, about that—"

He didn't get the chance to finish what he was going to say.

The sound of Noah's name being called over the PA system jolted both of them to attention. Annie immediately recognized the strident female voice as it came over the loudspeakers again, demanding that Noah Davis report to the emcee's station.

Annie glanced at Noah in confusion. "I didn't know Claudia was coming tonight."

He let out an aggravated sigh. "Neither did I."

They climbed out of the booth. Annie turned to see their printed photos sticking out of the machine. She quickly grabbed them and stuffed them into the back pocket of her jeans before following him as he headed for the sound system area where Claudia stood alone, scowling when she spotted him. That look went even colder when she noticed Annie trailing along too.

"What do you think you're doing?" Noah demanded, his deep voice calm but stern.

Claudia's hands fisted on the hips of her skirted, jewel-toned suit. "I suppose I should ask you the same thing."

"What are you talking about?"

"Our daughter, Noah." Claudia stepped closer. "I'm talking about the fact that she seems to enjoy defying me at every turn lately."

"What's that got to do with me? And why couldn't this conversation have waited until we could have it in private?"

Claudia's mouth thinned. "I'm sure you'd prefer that. Heaven forbid anyone here should hear us and see you as anything less than perfect."

"I don't care what anyone thinks of me," he countered. "What I do care about is protecting Lainey."

"Yes, I've noticed. You've also managed to make her hate me simply for trying to do what's right for the health of this school. Do you have any idea how it looks to a child when her father deliberately circumvents and sabotages her mother the way you've been doing with all of these fundraisers?"

Noah shook his head. "None of this is an effort to sabotage you or hurt your relationship with Lainey. Annie and I are simply trying to help the kids have their activities and their prom."

"Annie and you," Claudia echoed, shooting daggers past him to where Annie stood a couple of paces away from them. "How convenient that you have someone to help champion your cause to steal Lainey away from me."

He scowled. "I'm not doing any such thing. Neither is Annie."

"That's not how it looks to me," she snapped back. "It's not how it looks to Lainey, either. All she can talk about is how happy you two are together. Don't think I can't see that for myself. The whole town is talking about you and your old girlfriend, back together at last."

Noah glanced at Annie, an apologetic look in his eyes. Then he swung back to face his ex-wife. "Say what you want about me, I don't care. But leave Annie out of this. She doesn't deserve any of your spite or anger, Claudia. Annie is my friend, that's all. End of story."

Annie's heart stumbled a little in her chest to hear him declare that with such firm resolve.

His friend.

That's all. End of story.

She knew she shouldn't feel so crushed by that, but she was. She hadn't come home to Crestpoint Beach looking to fall in love with Noah again—if she'd ever stopped loving him at all—but she did love him.

And he considered her nothing more than a friend.

He couldn't have stated it more clearly than he had just now—to the woman who had once been his wife.

Annie lowered her head, suddenly feeling like an intruder, or worse, an unwanted bystander.

"Excuse me," she murmured, turning to step away.

"Annie," Noah said. He frowned, looking about as miserable as she felt. "You don't have to go."

"Yes, I do," she insisted. "You and Claudia need to have this conversation, and I need to go check in with Hannah."

"Annie, wait—"

She couldn't. Her face was flooding with heat and her throat was tight with emotion. She hurried out of the gymnasium and didn't slow her pace until she pushed open the girls' restroom door and felt it swing closed behind her.

It creaked open a few moments later, and Annie turned to find Hannah in the restroom with her.

"What just happened? You look like you're about to cry."

"No, I'm fine." Annie vigorously shook her head, even as her eyes welled with tears. "I'm okay."

"No, you're not." Hannah frowned. "I saw you and Noah talking to Claudia Harrow. Did she say something nasty to you?"

"No," Annie said, swiping at her wet cheeks. "It wasn't her. I don't care about anything she says to me."

Annie wasn't upset about Claudia. She understood Noah's ex was just hurt and jealous because Annie was forming a bond with Lainey. Maybe she had crossed a boundary, but not intentionally. She truly did not want to drive a wedge between Claudia and Lainey. She had no wish to complicate that relationship or to give Noah a harder time negotiating his relationship with Lainey, either.

As much as Annie's heart was hurting for herself now, she hurt just as much for the feeling that in rekindling her friendship with Noah, she was tearing all of them apart.

Hannah stared at her in mounting concern. "Did Noah do something, Annie? Honey, please tell me what happened."

"I will," she said, collecting herself as best she could. "Right now, I just want to be alone. I want to go home."

CHAPTER 12

It had been four days since the fundraiser at the high school and Noah hadn't seen Annie even once.

He tried to call her multiple times, attempting to apologize for Claudia's ambush and her harsh, undeserved words toward Annie. He couldn't blame her for leaving the fundraiser without explanation while he'd been busy trying to defuse the situation with Claudia in the gymnasium. Deep down, he worried that it was something more than simply his ex-wife's cutting words that pushed Annie away. His concern was swiftly intensifying into real fear that he was losing her all over again.

All of his calls went straight to voicemail. He sent her text messages, asking her to call him when she got the chance, but she only sent him a brief reply, stating that she was busy with other things that needed her attention and she would talk to him when her schedule settled down again.

Noah wasn't proud of it, but he had actually swung by the beach house after work one day, hoping to find her there so they could talk in person instead of briefly over text. Annie hadn't answered when he knocked. In fact, it appeared no one had been at the house for days. There were no tracks in the sand nor any noticeable ongoing changes to the beach house since he'd last seen it.

He had considered popping in at the Gift Emporium or at Frank Taylor's house to talk with Hannah, but respect for Annie's wishes forced him to draw the line at pumping her family for information when she had made it obvious that she either wasn't interested or wasn't ready to talk with him.

The waiting and not knowing was driving him to distraction. He felt himself going through the motions during his classes all week. Typically, he loved engaging with his students, asking questions, coming up with new learning experiments, and doing what he could to make biology interesting to teenagers. Instead, nearly all he could think about was Annie and how much he missed her.

It took forever for his free period to arrive, and rather than visit with Henry as he usually did, he chose to stay in his classroom. He grabbed his phone and checked for messages from Annie. There were none. He was about to send yet another one to her when a knock on the door jamb of his open office prompted him to look up.

"Hey, Dad. Are you busy?"

"Lainey." He checked the time on his phone and frowned as she strode into the room and slid into one of the seat in the front row. "What are you doing here? Shouldn't you be in the cafeteria having lunch with your friends now?"

"I ate a protein bar at my desk last period," she said with a shrug. "I hear the fundraisers were a big success."

"Yes, they were. Between the car washes and sale at school, we've nearly hit our big goal. If we can do another event with similar success, we should be able to put on the prom and bring back the clubs that were going to be cut."

"That's great," Lainey said, her tone hesitant. "But I know we're running out of time to save the prom."

Noah frowned, hearing the disappointment in her voice. "We'll figure something out."

"Do you and Annie have another plan?"

"No. Not yet." He glanced away, picking up a pile of tests and tapping them into a neat stack. "Don't worry about the dance. I've got a whole list of things left to try."

Lainey stared at him intently. "Are you all right, Dad? You seem different this week."

"Do I?"

He tried to play it casual, but her hazel gaze only further narrowed on him. "Are you depressed?"

Noah couldn't help but chuckle a little at the seriousness of her question. He didn't want her to worry about him when she needed to focus on herself. She was still grounded at Claudia's house this week, and he knew that navigating her relationship with her mother was plenty for Lainey to deal with. The last thing he wanted was for her to worry over the mess he was making of his personal life.

"I'm fine," he told her, even though he didn't feel fine so long as Annie was gone and not communicating with him.

Lainey crossed her arms in front of her, a look of regret on her youthful face. "I know Mom went to the fundraiser here at the school that night. I heard she was really mad, too."

Noah sighed, knowing he should have realized that Lainey would've heard about what happened. Word traveled fast in a small town, even faster in a small high school. Plenty of students had been around to witness when Claudia snapped at him and Annie.

"Did Mom get you in trouble with Annie? Is that why you've been so sad lately?"

Leave it to his daughter to see right through him. He slowly shook his head. "I don't think I can put the blame on your mom. I may have messed things up all on my own, unfortunately."

Lainey tilted her head. "Some of my friends told me they saw Annie come out of the girls' room with tears in her eyes."

"They said that?" Noah had no idea. Now, his concern for Annie increased tenfold. As did his need to see her again and do whatever he had to in order to make things right with her.

"Was Mom upset with you and Annie because she was angry at me over sneaking out to the car wash with Mason?" Lainey's face crumpled a bit. "I hope I'm not the reason she was mean to you and Annie."

"You're not, sweetheart. Your mom is just...protective when it comes to you."

He didn't want to point fingers or shine a bad light on Claudia, which was a bit hard to do given the intensity of the situation the other night. Claudia had been out of line snapping at him and Annie in public the way she had. She could've spoken to him privately and calmly, but instead she'd lashed out, even dragging Annie into her public spectacle. For that, it would be difficult to forgive Claudia.

"You say Mom's protective, but I think you mean she's jealous. She's jealous of Annie because I've been spending time with you and her. Together. She thinks we're going to be this whole new family, and she's going to be left behind."

Noah couldn't help but smile, despite the weight of his worries where he and Annie were concerned. "How'd you get so smart and grown up, kid?"

"I don't know."

He chuckled, getting up to move around to the front of his desk. He leaned on the edge, standing across from his daughter. He was pretty sure that Lainey was right about her mother's insecurities and fears. Claudia wanted to be involved and informed. If she felt she was being shut out of the loop involving her own daughter, it was only her reflex to push back or overreact.

Despite the tension between him and Claudia, Noah would never keep Lainey from her. Their daughter needed both of them. He only hoped that in time Claudia would learn to relax some of the iron grip she seemed to hold on Lainey and everything else around her.

"Your mom loves you very much," he assured her. "She just shows love a little differently sometimes."

Lainey rolled her eyes. "I know she does. I just wish she wouldn't worry about stuff like that. She's acting like Annie is filling out adoption paperwork for me," she said, laughing softly as she shook her head.

Noah chuckled too. For all the things that went wrong in his marriage to Claudia Harrow, they couldn't have done anything more right than the impressive young woman seated in front of him now. Lainey was a source of pride and joy to both of them, a reminder that even the hardest things in life can end up bringing the deepest happiness.

"So, have you talked to Annie, Dad?" Lainey asked, her expression softening slightly.

"No, I haven't." He shook his head as he drew his hand through his hair, wishing that he had better news to share with her on that front. "Annie texted me a few days ago that she's busy with some other things right now. I'm sure we'll be talking about all of this soon."

"You don't sound sure. You sound really sad." Lainey

sighed, wilting a little as she looked at him. "Did you guys break up?"

"Break up? Where'd you get that idea?" He shook his head. "We're just friends, kiddo."

"Just friends? Seriously, Dad?" Her brows rose. "You and Annie seem like more than friends to me. You guys act like you're in love with each other."

He sat back, stunned to realize his daughter could see something he'd been trying to deny for weeks. Trying, and failing.

Lainey huffed out a breath. "I don't know what happened, but you need to fix it, Dad. Annie's great. She seems good for you, too. I haven't seen you this happy in a long time, and I don't want you to lose her. I don't want you alone, especially because..." She trailed off, her words getting caught in her throat as she dropped her gaze.

"Because what?"

"Because I'll be graduating and going off to college soon. I can tell you don't like the weeks I'm at Mom's. You get lonely. When I go off to college, I'll only see you every once in a while. I just don't want you to feel that alone for so long."

Noah moved toward her, reaching out to place his hand on her shoulder, coaxing her to look up at him. "I will be just fine, Lainey. I promise I'll try to work things out with Annie, but the last thing I want you to worry about when you go off to college is me."

"I know. It's just...I can tell you guys would be good for each other."

"Come here," he said, drawing her up from the desk and into his embrace. She leaned forward, squeezing him tightly as she rested her cheek against his chest. Noah dropped a kiss on the top of her head. "I love you, sweetheart."

"Love you, too, Dad."

"I take it you kind of like Annie, too?"

Lainey nodded before lifting her head to look up at him, a warm smile crossing her lips. "She's awesome. I can also tell she makes you happy, and that's the most important thing. Just don't mess it up," she warned him playfully.

Noah chuckled as he cupped the back of her head gently, holding her close. If things worked out between him and Annie, it would help if Lainey liked her. He didn't think he could be with someone who didn't have a healthy, loving relationship with his child. Annie had already given him a glimpse of who she was with Lainey, and seeing them interact so easily had only made him love Annie more.

Lainey had been right about that. He was in love with Annie.

He only prayed he'd have the chance to tell her, and that she might feel even a little bit of love for him, too.

After the days of silence and avoidance, he had his doubts.

He drew Lainey out of his embrace and stared at the incredible young woman she was becoming. "You think it'll be too awful if I make you sit next to me in the cafeteria for a quick lunch?"

She grinned. "Not too awful."

He smiled back at her. "Good. Let's go, then. I'm starving."

CHAPTER 13

*A*nnie carried her suitcase up the steps of the beach house veranda early the next afternoon.

She had been away for the past three days, interviewing with a large interior design firm in Jacksonville. The offer to meet had been one of several that had hit her email from various firms since she'd been back in Crestpoint Beach. She hadn't been motivated to pursue any of them, but when she'd come home from the fundraiser, upset and hurting, she'd fired off a reply stating she might be interested in seeing what the firm had to say.

As it turned out, they'd had a lot to say. They flew her out to interview with the two senior partners of the firm, then spent a day showing her around the city and touring just a few of the many high-profile projects they had in mind for Annie if she signed on with them. She had to admit, she was impressed. Then, they'd presented her with their offer. Annie still couldn't believe the huge sum they'd proposed.

The full package was life-changing. A large salary plus commissions. A company-paid, high-rise condo right in the heart of Jacksonville. Extensive benefits and the potential of one day working her way up to partner in the firm. It was everything she'd ever dreamed of and more.

It was also more than three hundred miles away from Crestpoint Beach.

The way her heart had been aching after she left the gymnasium earlier that week, the distance should have been tempting all on its own. For part of her, it was. She needed some time and space to sort out her feelings, including the grief that still clung to her following Derek's death. That particular pain was lessening since she'd been home with her family, but closing the door on that chapter of her life still wasn't easy.

Falling back in love with Noah had only opened a new ache inside her.

It was that pain that had sent her to the interview in Jacksonville. Now, she had to decide if it was enough to keep her there permanently.

Stepping into the beach house, she couldn't help but feel a sense of pride for all that she and Hannah had accomplished. There was still furniture to add and miscellaneous pieces needed to tie everything together into a finished project, but even without all of the necessary final touches, the big old house felt like a home. *Her home.*

She had actually been considering Hannah's idea to open the grand Victorian as a bed-and-breakfast. The idea that had seemed so outrageous when her sister first mentioned it had been taking shape in Annie's mind...in her heart as well.

There was just so much to consider.

Annie knew the best place for thinking was always the beach, so she dropped her bag and went upstairs to change into a pair of shorts and a T-shirt, then grabbed her flip-flops and headed out onto the sand for a long walk.

She strolled toward the town's lighthouse, and found herself smiling as she approached the black-and-white tower. Her father was on a beach chair in the sand beside the old light he used to manage before the park service took it over. The light's afternoon shadow provided a shady spot amid the white sand and tall seagrass, and that was where Frank Taylor sat, looking out over the water.

"I guess I shouldn't be surprised to find you here," she said as she approached him.

He glanced over at her and smiled fondly. "Old habits die hard."

"Well, this is a good one to keep," she said. "Want some company?"

"Of course. I'll even give you my chair." He started to get up, moving slowly.

"No, Dad. You sit. I'd rather plop right here on the sand, anyway."

She did just that, seating herself at his side. A few sailboats were out on the water, taking advantage of the calm sea and moderate breeze. Annie was content to simply sit with her father for a few moments and stare out at the beauty of the ocean.

"It's so peaceful here. I had forgotten how much."

"Balm for whatever ails you," he said. "I used to come out here and sit for hours at a time after your mom passed."

Annie reached over and placed her hand on his forearm. "Does it ever get...easier?"

Her question was vague, but she was confident he would know what she meant. They had ventured down a similar path, one of grief and despair and learning to carry on afterward.

"It does, honey. Time and the love of people around you are the best healers," he told her with a small smile. "The grief will always be a part of you, but the heart is a resilient organ. It mends. Eventually, it mends enough to open itself to life, and love, again."

Annie leaned her head against his arm and simply breathed for a few moments. The burden on her heart over Derek's death and her surviving him to carry on was made heavier by the guilt she'd been carrying since the day of the accident.

She swallowed, searching for her voice. "I was supposed to go with Derek that day, Dad. We were going to ride together on his motorcycle to the client meeting, but I...I backed out. The weather looked bad, and I didn't want to risk it. Derek got upset with me, and he went without me."

"Oh, Annie." Her father heaved a slow sigh and shifted so that he could gather her in his arms. He kissed the top of her head, his lips lingering on her hair for a long moment. "I'm sorry, sweetheart. I'm sorry about Derek, but I can't be sorry that you weren't on that bike with him. And you shouldn't feel guilty over that, either."

"But I do." She drew out of his comforting embrace and looked up at him. "I feel guilty for the fact that I'm here and he's not. I feel even more guilty because since coming back home, I've been happier than ever before."

At least, she *was* happier. The time she'd been spending with Noah had been some of the best days of her life. Not even the hurt of his rejection at the fundraiser could totally dim the fun memories she had made with him again.

"You're allowed to feel happiness, Annie. You're allowed to love again, too."

"Did you...after Mom?"

He went quiet, his gaze distant and tender with reflection. "My Ginny was everything to me. She was my best friend and companion—my heart and soul—for a decade before I lost her. After she was gone, I had you girls to raise. You and Hannah were all I needed for a long time. You still are, most days. But I dated now and then over the years. I knew your mom would want me to find love again. Maybe one day I will."

Annie smiled at him. "You and Mom had something pretty special. I recognized that even as a kid."

"Yes, we did. That kind of love only comes along once in a lifetime." He patted her hand. "I think you know that as well as anyone."

She exhaled, knowing he was talking about Noah and her. Until a few days ago, she would have agreed with him. She and Noah did have something special. She had allowed herself to believe it was still there, seventeen years after they went their separate ways. Her heart still wanted to believe that, even though Noah evidently felt differently.

"Aren't you going to tell me how the interview went, honey?"

She turned to look at him. "It went really well. Maybe too well. I got the job."

"I knew you would." His smile didn't quite reach his wise blue eyes. "When do you start?"

"Three weeks from now."

He nodded, turning his gaze back out to the waves. "Jacksonville is a long way away from Crestpoint Beach."

"Yes, it is." The distance seemed to expand in her mind

every minute since she'd signed the contract. "I'll probably only get to come back home once every few months or so. I promise, I will. I don't ever want to go so long without seeing you and Hannah again."

"And Noah?" he asked. "What does he think about all of this?"

"I haven't told him." She sighed. "To be honest, I haven't spoken to him at all since before I left to take the interview."

"You haven't spoken?" He looked at her with furrowed brows. "You two have been practically inseparable since you came home. To be honest, honey, I thought the two of you were picking up right where you left off all those years ago."

"I did, too, Dad." She lifted her shoulder and slowly shook her head. "Now, I'm just…confused."

"About you and Noah?"

"Yes, about him. About everything."

He made a thoughtful sound. "You think things are going to get any clearer for you if you move away to Jacksonville?"

"I don't know, but maybe I need to find out."

"Running away never solved a thing, sweetheart. It just sends your troubles down the road along with you. Sooner or later, you have to face them."

She knew he was right. Her father always had a clear-eyed view of things, a skill she'd often credited to his work manning the light that had guided weary souls to safe harbor for decades. If only it were so easy for her to see her way through the heartache and confusion that gripped her since she last saw Noah.

"I fell in love with him again, Dad." She spoke the words quietly, toying with a small shell she plucked out of the sand. "Seventeen years after he broke my heart, I let myself fall right back in all over again."

Her father's gnarled hand came to rest lightly on the back of her head. He stroked her hair. "I don't think you ever truly stopped loving Noah Davis. I know he never stopped loving you."

She glanced up, frowning. "At the fundraiser for the school a few nights ago, Claudia showed up and started an argument with her. She brought me into it and Noah told her we were, and I quote, 'just friends, nothing more, end of story.' He told me practically the same thing before then, but I didn't want to believe it."

"And now you do? Do you actually believe Noah feels anything less for you than you feel for him?"

"I don't know what to believe. All I know is I'm afraid to let him hurt me again. I had never felt so abandoned and lost as I did that night he stood me up for the prom. But then he said those things to his ex-wife in front of me, and I felt like that abandoned eighteen-year-old girl again. I felt like a fool."

"Well, honey, I've been away from affairs of the heart for a long time now, but one thing I do know is that the boy who let you leave him in order to pursue your dreams did it because he loved you and wanted the best for you. Noah loved you enough to let you go."

She drew back, stunned. "You knew?"

Her father gave her a remorseful nod. "You were gone away to college about a week before he stopped by the house looking like he had the weight of the world on his shoulders. He told me how awful he felt for the way he'd behaved, lacking the courage to tell you in person so he ended up wounding you even more deeply instead by standing you up."

"Why didn't you tell me any of this before?"

"It wasn't my place, Annie. Still isn't, but I hate seeing you torn up like this."

She shook her head, unable to find anger for Noah's actions or her father's in keeping Noah's secret from her. It was time for her to let go of the past and move forward. She had to figure out who she was going to be, especially now that Noah was out of the equation.

"It's okay, Dad. I'm glad I know now, but it doesn't change the fact that I need to move on. I need to figure out what my future is going to look like."

"I understand, sweetheart. I'm not going to hold you back from doing whatever your heart tells you is right...even if that takes you away from Crestpoint Beach."

Just hearing those words made it all feel real. Could she leave her hometown again when it already felt like a part of her? Could she really leave the beach house and all of the dreams she and Hannah had for it? Could she truly leave Noah behind for good?

They were questions that had been churning in her mind since she'd boarded the plane for her interview. When she'd signed the contract in Jacksonville, it had seemed like she'd answered them, but now she wondered.

Either way, she had three weeks to prepare for her move. There were things she needed to do before then, including one big decision that had been weighing on her for the past nine months.

"I'm going to head back," she said, rising to her feet. "I haven't unpacked my suitcase, and I have a few things I need to take care of back at the house."

"All right, honey." Her father smiled up at her. "I'm going to stay here for a bit longer and watch the waves."

She bent down and kissed his grizzled cheek. "Thank you for talking with me. You always know just what to say."

He chuckled softly. "I'm here for you anytime, Annie. I love you."

"I love you, too, Dad."

With a warmth she felt down to her soul, she turned away and headed back up the sand for the beach house with a new sense of resolve.

CHAPTER 14

*L*ainey burst into Noah's classroom before the first bell rang for the start of Friday's school day. "Have you heard?"

He glanced up from reviewing his lesson plan. Her cheeks were flushed with color, her eyes bright with excitement. She was practically bouncing.

"Have I heard what?"

"Prom!" she exclaimed. "It's back on. Mom just told me this morning."

"How can that be?" Noah couldn't hide his confusion. "Did your mom and the board have a change of heart or something?"

"Even better," Lainey said, grinning. "Someone in town donated all the money we needed to host the prom and to fund the clubs that were cut. Isn't that amazing news?"

"That's incredible news," he agreed. "Was it one of the local businesses who made the donation?"

Lainey shrugged. "I don't know. Mom said the donor

wants to stay anonymous. Whoever it is, they're my new hero because I'm going to prom!"

Noah chuckled as she twirled in front of his desk, elation radiating off her. She stopped abruptly and gave him a wide-eyed smile. "I have to go tell Mason and my friends. Bye, Dad!"

She dashed out to the hallway, leaving Noah laughing under his breath. He was delighted to see his daughter so happy, and he was excited for the rest of the students who had been looking forward to the annual celebration with as much anticipation as Lainey. The fact that the generous donation had also funded his science club and the others facing cuts only made the news that much sweeter.

There was only one person he wanted to share the surprise announcement with, but he was still waiting on Annie's promised call. He had been trying to give her the space she evidently needed, but it was proving harder than he imagined to get through the hours and days without his best friend.

He missed her. It didn't feel right not being able to pick up the phone and hear her voice, or to see her in person.

It had been less than a week since she'd shut him out of her life and he was miserable. How long would he be able to go on like this, waiting and hoping she would come back to him?

Those thoughts stayed with him for the duration of his day. Once his final period ended and the students filed out of his classroom to go home, he collected his things and headed out to his Jeep.

He wanted Annie to hear about the miracle windfall. She deserved to share in the excitement, too. More than that, Noah wanted to share the news with her personally.

He also wanted to reassure himself that things between

them could go back to normal, that he hadn't lost her completely.

He drove to the beach house and found her outside, tending the flower beds below the veranda. She looked adorable in her floppy sun hat and gardening apron, which she wore over a summer tank top and loose-fitting, faded denim cutoffs.

Crouched on her knees in the sand, she pulled some weeds from deep within the pink flowers, glancing up as Noah strode toward her on the narrow, bricked walkway.

"Hi, Annie."

"Noah." She swallowed visibly, setting the wilted clump of weeds down beside her as she removed her gardening gloves and stood up. "What are you doing here?"

It wasn't a cold demand. Far from it. Her voice was quiet and uncertain. Her gaze held his as she inhaled a deep breath.

He shifted on his feet. "I just…I wanted to see you, Annie. I hope you don't mind me dropping by like this."

"No. I don't mind." She glanced away from him for a moment and shook her head. "I'm sorry I haven't called you back yet."

"It's okay, don't worry about it. You said you were busy, and I can see that you have been. The house looks amazing. It's easily the most beautiful place on the beach now." He smiled at her, proud of everything she had accomplished. "If you and Hannah do decide to open it as a B&B, you're going to be sold out every week."

Something in her blue eyes dimmed. "Why are you here, Noah?"

Because I've missed you and I need you. Because I couldn't go another minute without seeing your face.

Because I love you, and always have.

All of those reasons welled up in his chest, but remained stuck in his throat when he saw the guardedness in her gaze. Just because she was politely talking to him now didn't mean she was allowing him back into her life. If he said the wrong thing, or pushed her in a direction she wasn't ready to go, she might never open that door to him again.

He cleared his throat. "I have some great news, and I wanted to be the one to tell you. The prom and the after-school clubs...they've been reinstated. Every single one of them."

She smiled. "The kids must be very happy about that."

"They're over the moon." He couldn't hold back his enthusiasm, either. "You should've seen Lainey when she came into my class this morning to tell me. Apparently, an anonymous donor contributed all of the funds that were needed to make up what the fundraisers hadn't been able to reach."

She let go of a slow breath and nodded. "I'm glad everything worked out for you...and the kids."

"You were the first person I wanted to tell. You're responsible for all of this, Annie."

"Me?" She seemed to draw back a little. "Why do you say that?"

"Because without you encouraging me to do something to save those events, I'm not sure I would've tried. We started the ball rolling with our fundraiser ideas. If we hadn't, that donor might never have come forward to help push us over the line."

"I'm sure something would've worked out," she said, turning away from him to pick up her gloves.

"Annie," he said, taking a step toward her. It was all he could do to resist the urge to draw her into his arms. "This victory belongs to you, too. You worked so hard to make this happen. We both did, together. I think we should celebrate it."

She glanced at him, wariness in her voice and in her eyes. "What do you mean?"

He took a fortifying breath. "Come to the prom with me. Let's do it over. Give me a chance to get it right this time."

She turned away again, her movements abrupt, as if she were moments from bolting from him. "Noah, I'm sorry. I don't think that's a good idea."

"I think it's a great idea. Please, let me try to make up for what I did wrong. I want to make everything up to you, if you'll let me."

When she faced him now, there was a sadness in her expression that threatened to break him. "Noah, I can't live in the past anymore. I have to put it behind me now…everything. I need to move forward with my life."

"That's what I'm talking about, too. Annie, I want us to start over—"

"I took a job in Jacksonville," she blurted out in a rush.

"What?" He couldn't disguise his shock. Or his disappointment. "When?"

"I flew out this week for the interview, and they made me an amazing offer. It's a large firm with an incredible client list. They tell me there's a good chance I can make partner in a few years."

Noah felt as if the ground had just opened up beneath him. "That's…wonderful news for you, Annie. How soon before you'd have to go?"

"I start in less than three weeks."

No decision left to be made, no conditions required to be met before she left to take this new opportunity. It was done. She was leaving Crestpoint Beach.

Again.

He stepped back, running his hand over his head. "I'm…

happy for you. I know you're going to be great. You have the whole world open in front of you, Annie. This is just…I'm surprised, that's all."

Blindsided, in fact. Suddenly his entire world felt knocked off-balance.

"I didn't mean to keep it from you, Noah." She swallowed, looking about as tormented as he felt. "I was going to tell you the next time we talked."

He waved his hand in a dismissive gesture. "It's all right. You don't owe me any explanations. You know I always want what's best for you, Annie. I want you to be happy."

"I want that for you, too," she murmured. "I'm sorry if I've made things difficult for you or Lainey with Claudia. I never wanted to make you feel you have to defend me or justify my presence in your life."

"You haven't done that. Please, don't ever think that. Nothing Claudia has said has anything to do with you. She is her own problem, and always has been."

He wanted to reach out to Annie, but she was already stepping farther away. She picked up her gardening tools and held them in front of her, putting more than distance between them.

Noah could hardly bear the idea that she would be leaving town in less than three weeks' time.

"Can we…see each other before you have to go? Just for lunch, or a coffee, or something."

A small crease formed between her brows as her lips turned down at the corners. "I don't think we should, Noah. I have a lot to get done between now and when I leave. But I'm sure we'll see each other around town."

"Yeah. I'm sure we will."

She nodded, still holding her tools against her like a shield.

"Well, I should get back to work while I have the last few hours of afternoon sunlight."

"Right," Noah said, emotion clawing at him. "I guess I'll see you around, Annie."

She stared at him, unblinking. "Goodbye, Noah."

He pivoted away from her and made the long walk back to his vehicle for what felt like it could be the last time.

CHAPTER 15

The energy around town the following week was impossible to miss.

With exactly seven days to go before the prom, the local florist had a sign in their front window advertising corsages and boutonnieres. The salon was promoting special pricing on hair and nails for prom-goers. Tuxedoed mannequins stood in the window at the menswear and tailoring shop, and there wasn't a boutique on Main Street that hadn't swapped out the usual parade of resort wear and other tourist-friendly clothing at the fronts of their stores in favor of sparkly, colorful gowns and cocktail dresses.

Annie walked into one of those boutiques on a Saturday morning, in search of a new outfit to wear for her first day of work at the new firm in a couple more weeks. It was a small store, but the walls were lined with beautiful dresses, skirts, blouses, and other fashion pieces. Racks of clothes and jewelry covered the wooden floor all the way toward the back of the store where the dressing rooms were located. Mainstream pop music lightly sounded out of speakers mounted in the top corners of the boutique.

More than a dozen high school girls were shopping inside, some trying dresses on with friends, others accompanied by their mothers. She couldn't help smiling at their palpable excitement. The giggles and lit-up faces helped lift some of the weight from her heart as she strolled through the boutique and began to browse for a skirt and jacket.

Her conversation with Noah at the beach house a few days earlier kept replaying in her mind. She knew her decision had taken him aback. Evidently, he'd expected they would simply keep going on as they had been, reunited friends who used to be something more, but now…what? She didn't know what she was to him. Maybe he didn't, either.

She'd been secretly hoping he'd give her a reason not to go to Jacksonville, but he hadn't. He had been his usual supportive self, more confident in her future than she was. She used to love that about him. She still did.

The problem was, she loved everything about Noah Davis, and living in the same town with him yet not sharing every part of her life with him was going to hurt too much for her to stay. At least, that's what she had told herself when she'd placed her signature on the contract in Jacksonville.

Now, she was beginning to think the pain of being in love with Noah was going to follow her no matter where she was.

Annie reached for a cute black skirt in her size on one of the racks near the dressing rooms. At the same time, the louvered door to one of the stalls squeaked open and a familiar voice called out in a loud whisper.

"Mom, I told you this green dress was gonna be too tight on me."

Annie winced at the sound of Lainey's voice and shrank

down a little, praying she would go unnoticed. No such luck. From the corner of her eye, she saw Claudia's auburn hair and sultry figure cutting a path right toward her. She had an assortment of pastel-colored gowns draped over her arm.

Their gazes collided, and Claudia's chin rose a notch in response. She looked about as uncomfortable with this unanticipated encounter as Annie felt. She would have expected the pair of them to shop for Lainey's dress at Claudia's own shop, the upscale Harrow's Cove, but it was obvious Oceanview Boutique was the shop of choice for their large inventory of glittery, frothy prom attire.

"Annie?" Lainey rushed up from behind and wrapped her arms around her without a moment's hesitation. "Where've you been? I haven't seen you in forever!"

"Hi, Lainey." Annie glanced at the girl's mother and gave her a polite, albeit awkward, smile. "Hello, Claudia."

"Hello."

Lainey looked positively giddy. "Did you hear the amazing news? We're having the prom this year after all!"

Annie couldn't help but share some of the girl's excitement. "That's wonderful, Lainey. I'm very happy for you."

"I'm trying to find the perfect dress. Can you help me, please?"

Annie knew the question was well-intentioned and innocent, but she felt a pang of sympathy for Claudia standing beside her in silence.

"Oh, I don't think you need me. It looks like you've got some beautiful options right here," Annie said, gesturing to the collection of dresses Claudia held.

"Let me see, Mom." Lainey pulled a few out of the group, gasping in delight at some and wrinkling her nose at others. "I like these three the best. Stay right here and I'll try them on!"

She dashed back into the dressing room and closed the door with a bang and a giggle.

"She's been beaming like this all week," Claudia remarked quietly. "I really had no idea how much the prom meant to her. Or to the rest of the students."

Annie nodded. "It's the social highlight of high school."

"Yes, it is." Claudia glanced at her. "Somewhere along the way, I'd lost sight of that fact. Maybe I am too focused on grooming her to be an adult, instead of letting her enjoy these years while she can."

Annie looked at her. "I know you haven't asked for my opinion, but I think Lainey's turning out just fine. She's fortunate to have a mother to watch out for her."

Something softened in Claudia's expression. "Thank you."

Annie nodded. "You're welcome. I'm sorry if my being back in town made you uncomfortable in any way. It truly wasn't my intention."

Claudia sighed. "I feel like I should be the one apologizing to you, Annie. It was wrong for me to lash out at you because of my own insecurities. It was wrong for me to lash out at Noah the way I did, too."

Annie smiled and shook her head. "It's okay. I know it must be complicated for all of you."

Just then, Lainey stepped out of the fitting room in one of the dresses. "Well, what do you think?"

Annie gasped quietly, astonished to see Lainey transformed from the T-shirts, jeans, and Converse tomboy she'd gotten to know these past weeks into a stunning young woman in the dark turquoise, strapless, tea-length gown. She held her reaction, allowing Lainey's mother to be the first to voice her opinion.

Claudia seemed equally moved. She brought her hand up

to her mouth and inhaled a short breath, her eyes glistening. "Oh, Lainey. You look absolutely stunning."

"Do I?" She glanced from her mother to Annie. "What do you think?"

"I agree with your mom one hundred percent. Absolutely stunning, Lainey."

The teen grinned, color rising into her cheeks. "I feel like a princess." She spun around a couple of times, letting the ankle-length skirt flare out around her. When she stopped, she dashed forward and gave her mother a kiss on the cheek. "Thank you for finding this one for me. I love it."

Claudia nodded, a rare tenderness in her normally reserved expression. "We'll have to find you a nice pair of shoes to go with it."

"Okay!" Lainey bounced on her bare feet before disappearing back into the fitting room.

Claudia looked at Annie. "My little girl is growing up right before my eyes."

"She's lovely, inside and out," Annie remarked. "You and Noah have raised a very special young woman."

"Thank you," Claudia said, a hint of emotion in her voice. "I can see why she's fond of you, Annie. I can see why Noah is, too."

Annie nodded, feeling a twinge of regret for the fact that she would soon be leaving both Noah and Lainey behind in just a couple more weeks. She wondered if there might have been a chance that she and Claudia could have mended things between them, too. Now, she would never know.

"Annie," Claudia whispered hesitantly. "I wanted to thank you for something else, too. Your donation to the school was incredibly generous. I know it was intended to be anonymous, but...well, Crestpoint Beach is a small town, and my colleagues are terrible at keeping secrets."

Annie returned her warm smile. "I'm glad I was able to help. I'd been holding on to the life insurance proceeds from my husband's death nine months ago, unable to spend it. I thought about it for a while, and I realized if some of the money could help bring a little joy to the kids here at home, I know Derek would've approved."

"I'm very sorry for your loss, Annie. I had no idea." Claudia slowly shook her head. "Crestpoint Beach must be very special to you."

"This is my hometown. I care about it, and the people who live here. I always have, and always will. I'm going to miss it terribly."

Claudia's fine brows pinched. "Are you leaving?"

"I was offered a job in Jacksonville. I start in a couple of weeks."

"Oh. Annie, I...I hope your decision to go doesn't have anything to do with me, or the things I've done or said." Claudia stared at her with sincere remorse.

"No. The decision was mine. I can't live in the past. I need to start moving forward."

"You can't do that here?"

"I thought I could, but things are different. I thought I had something here that I don't anymore."

"You're talking about Noah."

Annie nodded. Maybe she should feel awkward admitting that to his ex-wife, especially after her rocky start with Claudia, but there was no hiding her sadness and confusion.

"You're still in love with him." Claudia stared at her in silent understanding. "You never stopped loving him, did you?"

"A part of me has always belonged to Noah," she admitted. "I don't think anything can change that."

"Not even moving to the other side of the state," Claudia pointed out. "Does he know?"

"Yes. I told him a few days ago."

Claudia frowned, her head tilted. "You haven't told him how you feel, have you?"

Annie shook her head. "I've been too afraid. He told me he wanted to be friends. He told you the same thing, too, that night of the fundraiser."

"Yes, that is what he said to me." Claudia's expression grew tender. "Annie, that man has been head over heels in love with you since grade school. I knew that when Noah and I got together. I knew it when he offered to marry me. But you're the woman he loves. You always have been."

Emotion climbed up her throat as she listened. "He's letting me go. When I told him I had taken the job, he wished me well. Then we said goodbye and he walked away."

"Because that's what he thought you wanted, I'm sure. That's what Noah does—the noble thing, no matter what it costs him. That's just who he is."

Annie couldn't argue about his goodness or his honorable nature. It was just hard to accept that whatever he felt for her evidently wasn't enough for him to make her stay. "He didn't fight for me, Claudia. Not the other day, not seventeen years ago, either."

"He wants what's best for *you*. Even if that doesn't include him." Claudia studied her, a look of sympathy in her gaze. "I don't think being apart is what either of you really want. But that's not for me to say."

Annie's eyes prickled with welling tears. She blinked them away, her thoughts churning as intensely as her emotions.

Claudia had given her a lot to think about, and there was no time to ponder it now because Lainey stepped out of the fitting room with her dress folded over her arm.

"Mom, you know what shoes I think would look amazing with this dress? That pair of black sandals with the thin ankle straps and little rhinestones on them at your shop."

"Oh, yes, you're right," Claudia replied, wrapping her arm around her daughter's shoulders. "Those would be a perfect choice, sweetheart."

Annie smiled at both of them, pleased to see their shared excitement and happiness. "You're going to look absolutely gorgeous, Lainey."

She beamed. "Will I see you there, Annie?"

"I don't think so," she said gently. "The prom is for students and faculty to enjoy. I would only be in the way."

"No, you wouldn't. Besides, my dad will want you there, for sure."

Annie slanted a glance at Claudia, but saw no jealousy or ill will in her eyes. Only silent understanding. "The important thing is that you and your friends have a great time at the dance. I'll be there in spirit."

Lainey seemed to wilt a bit, but then she stepped forward and gave Annie a hug. "I hope you change your mind."

Annie smiled. "Have fun, all right?"

She bobbed her head, then moved back to join her mom. Claudia smiled. "I hope you'll change your mind, too, Annie."

She wasn't only talking about the prom. Her kindness today had been a surprise. A welcome one.

Her comments about Noah stayed with Annie long after Claudia and Lainey had left the boutique to continue their shopping.

CHAPTER 16

*P*rom night arrived in what felt like no time to Noah.

It was something of a miracle that everything had come together so quickly, from the music and catering to the decorations.

The students, faculty, and parents had all pitched in together, making what would normally take months to plan instead take shape in the space of a couple weeks.

That the prom was happening at all was due to the generosity of the anonymous donor who had given everyone the incentive—and the financial means—to pull the many details together in such a short amount of time.

Noah felt a sense of pride as he approached the packed gymnasium. Music and chatter from inside poured out through the open gym doors into the hallway. Swirling blue light flashed from all corners of the space, which was filled with excited teenagers and the team of parent and teacher chaperones overseeing the event.

He smiled as he entered the gym to take his place among the rest of his colleagues. The student committee had gone with an underwater theme.

Blue-tinted lighting filled the space, and glowing jellyfish lanterns hung suspended in the air above the dance floor in the middle of the gym as students swayed and jumped around to the pop music playing from the DJ's booth toward the back wall.

Blue, green, and purple streamers hung down toward the crowd from the ceiling, along with balloons and sheer curtains that sectioned off the DJ booth and concession area, which had tables full of cups with punch, frosted sea creature shaped cookies, and other aquatic-themed treats.

He plucked a crab-shaped cookie from the refreshment table and ate it while he watched the kids dance, laugh, and snap photos together.

Annie should be with him, too. The success of the prom was as much her victory as anyone else's.

As he'd told her that afternoon at her house—the last time he'd seen her—it was because of her determination and creativity that he had even considered trying to do something to circumvent the board's budget cuts. She deserved to celebrate this and to see what her efforts had done to give the students a night they would remember for the rest of their lives.

More than that, however, he just plain missed her.

As quickly as the time leading up to prom had passed, the nearly two weeks without Annie in his life had felt like an eternity.

The idea of her leaving the hometown for good had put an ache in his chest that hadn't let up for a moment since she'd informed him she had taken the job in Jacksonville. In only another week, she'd be gone.

As much as he loved teaching in Crestpoint Beach, if he didn't have Lainey to consider, he would already have his resume in at every school he could find in the city or nearby.

His entire life had been built in this town, but his heart belonged to Annie. That was never going to change.

If he had to wait until Lainey was on her own before he could follow Annie to Jacksonville, that's what he would do. He only hoped Annie would be willing to let him back into her heart. If she found another man who could love her better in the meantime, Noah would deal with that heartbreak when it came.

"Hey, Dad!" Lainey ran up to his side from another area of the gym, her hand linked with Mason's. She let go of her date to throw her arms around Noah. "Doesn't everything look amazing tonight?"

He chuckled, setting her away from him so he could admire the young woman he hardly recognized with her brown hair swept up in a high ponytail and soft tendrils styled into delicate curls to frame her pretty face. She wore a little makeup tonight, just enough to emphasize her long lashes and to add a bit of color to her eyelids and cheeks. Pale pink gloss slicked her lips.

He reached out and took her hand, playfully giving her a spin in front of him. The strapless turquoise dress she wore was stunning, yet youthful, with just a hint of grown-up elegance. He didn't know how she was able to walk in the strappy sandals she wore, but she handled herself with a grace that surprised him.

As he looked at her, it struck him how his little girl wasn't so little anymore. "Lainey, you are breathtaking."

"Thanks, Dad."

Noah held his hand out to her anxious date, who was fidgeting with the tight collar of his bow-tied tuxedo shirt. "Mason, you clean up pretty well yourself."

"Thank you, Mr. Davis." The boy shook his hand, grinning. "I like your suit, too. Nice tie."

Noah felt confined in the dark charcoal-colored jacket and slacks, which he usually reserved for funerals. He'd livened it up for this event with a colorful tie sporting the Milky Way galaxy on it.

Lainey beamed at Mason. "Let's go dance. This song is one of my favorites."

"Mm-kay," the boy agreed, taking her hand.

"Have fun, you two," Noah told them as they dashed back out to the dance floor.

Noah watched for a while, a smile crossing his face as Lainey jumped around with Mason to the upbeat song, laughter bubbling from her. That was exactly how he wanted to see his daughter. He always wanted her to be that happy.

As he enjoyed the moment, he saw Claudia approaching in his peripheral vision. Bracing himself for the usual clash with his ex, he turned to face her.

To his astonishment, she was smiling. More than smiling, she looked positively delighted.

"Hi, Noah."

"Claudia." He nodded in greeting, unsure he could trust the sense of peace that seemed to surround her. "I didn't realize you'd be here tonight."

She gave him a sheepish smile. "I wasn't sure I'd be welcome."

"Of course, you're welcome to attend. You're on the board, and you're also a parent."

"I mean, I wasn't sure you'd want me here."

His brows knit. "I don't mind at all," he said, meaning it wholeheartedly. "I also know it's going to mean a lot to Lainey that you came."

Claudia's smile relaxed as she gazed out at the dance floor. "Isn't our daughter beautiful?"

"Yes, she is. And she's having such a great time tonight."

They watched all of the kids on the dance floor for a few moments, then Claudia turned to him again. "Noah, I'm... sorry for the way I've behaved. Not just lately, but for a long time. It wasn't easy for me after our divorce. I know that's no excuse, but failing at something creates a lot of stress for me."

"I know," he said, reaching out to place his hand on her shoulder. "Divorce wasn't something I ever wanted for myself either. I think we can both agree that it was for the best. We're both happier being apart."

She nodded, studying him for a long moment. "You're a wonderful father to our daughter. You always have been. I think I've been a little envious of how easy your relationship is with her. I try so hard to be a good mother, but I can never seem to have the closeness you and Lainey share."

Noah quirked a wry smile. "Maybe you shouldn't try so hard, Claudia. Sometimes you have to get out of your own way."

She laughed softly. "You're right. And I'm trying to let up... on a lot of things."

"I'm glad to hear that." He gave her shoulder a light squeeze before he drew his hand away. "I know you excel at anything you really put your mind to, so I imagine you'll do just fine with Lainey going forward."

She gazed out at the dance floor again. "Thank you for letting her come to my house tonight so I could help her get ready. I know it's technically your week with her, but we had fun getting dressed up together. She even let me do her hair and makeup."

Noah nodded. "It was no problem at all. You did a great job for her. She looks incredible."

Claudia cleared her throat. "I would've thought I'd see Annie here tonight."

"I don't think she's coming," he said, hoping the true depth of his disappointment didn't show in his face. "She took a new job out of town. She's going to be moving away soon."

"You don't sound happy about that."

"I'm not," he admitted.

"Then, what are you doing here, Noah?"

"Excuse me?"

Claudia's smile was tender. "Go after her. Tell her you're still in love with her. Don't let her leave without telling her how you feel. You already made that mistake once. I don't want to see you do it again."

He frowned, taken aback to be receiving advice about Annie from the woman he'd once been married to. "It doesn't matter how I feel. She has an amazing job waiting for her. She has a shiny new future to begin somewhere else. I don't want to hold her back from any of that. I couldn't do it before, either."

"I know you couldn't, Noah. But maybe you should let Annie decide that for herself."

Even though a part of him knew Claudia was right, he shook his head. "I'm her past. What can I offer her, even if she did decide to stay?"

"The one thing she's always wanted more than anything else. You."

He stared at her in confusion. "Why are you telling me all of this, Claudia?"

"Because I've known all along how much Annie Taylor meant to you. And after speaking with her myself earlier this week while Lainey and I were shopping for dresses, I realized how much you mean to her, too." Claudia hesitated, as if she had more on her mind. She lowered her voice for his ears only. "There is something else you need to know. It was Annie who made the anonymous donation to save the prom and the after-school clubs."

"What?" Noah reeled at the news. "How?"

"She used some of the proceeds from her husband's life insurance to pay for what was unmet by the fundraisers the two of you held."

Noah staggered back on his heels. "She did that for Crestpoint Beach?"

"I think she did it for you, too. She's in love with you, Noah."

"Why didn't she tell me any of this?"

Claudia arched her brows. "Because she's afraid of getting hurt again."

He released a sigh and ran his hand over his jaw. "I'm an idiot. I told her I wanted us to be friends. I do want us to be friends, but what I should've told her is that I love her."

Claudia smiled. "Maybe you're not too late."

Was she right? Could he fix things with Annie? Could he correct not only the mistake he'd made with her in the past, but the one he was making now?

Hope exploded inside him at the thought. He didn't know if Annie would forgive him, or if she truly wanted him in her life now, but he had to try.

"Thank you, Claudia." He leaned forward and pecked her on the cheek. "I can't stay another minute. I have to go find Annie right now."

Claudia nodded, laughing softly. "Good luck, Noah."

CHAPTER 17

"Do you really think this is a good idea, Hannah?"

Annie peered out the windshield of her Toyota at the crowded parking lot outside the high school. Music from inside the gymnasium carried all the way outside to where she and her sister had just parked.

"I think it's an excellent idea," Hannah said, turning to look at her from the passenger seat. She brought her fingers up her to lips as she smiled, her eyes filled with encouragement and affection. "You look amazing, sis."

"Thanks. So do you."

"Then, let's do this!" Hannah giggled, reaching for the door handle and climbing out of the car.

Annie drew in a steadying breath, the fitted bodice of her sky-blue cocktail dress hugging her ribs as she inhaled. She turned off the engine and placed the key fob in her small evening bag, then stepped out of the Corolla to join Hannah outside. She shut the door behind her and stood for a moment in her champagne-colored heels, staring at the glow of lights as the rhythmic pound of pop music emanated from the prom going on in the gym.

She hadn't been so nervous since another prom night seventeen years ago.

That night had ended in heartbreak. She wasn't sure this one wouldn't have a similar outcome. All she did know was that if she walked into that gymnasium now, she wasn't going to leave until Noah Davis knew everything she'd been carrying in her heart all these years.

Tonight, she would leave nothing on the field—including her pride.

Hannah walked over in her lavender dress and took Annie's hand. "Ready?"

Annie smiled, doing all she could to tamp down her nerves. "Ready or not, right?"

Hannah laughed. "You've got this."

Annie only wished she had her sister's confidence. She'd been doing a lot of thinking over the past week, a lot of soul searching. She'd weighed a lot of heavy decisions—ones that were already in motion even before she took the first step toward the packed gymnasium tonight.

Now, it was time to put her heart out in the open.

She just hoped it wasn't about to get crushed.

Hannah opened the exterior door to the school and Annie walked inside. Chaperones checking IDs nodded to her and Hannah, recognizing the sisters without the need to make them pause inside the doors.

Annie wasn't sure if it was her heart or the music that throbbed so powerfully in her chest as she and Hannah walked further into the hallway.

At the same time, a tall, athletic man in a dark suit came

rushing out of the gymnasium as though he were running to put out a fire.

Noah.

He stopped short the instant his gaze lit on Annie.

She froze, too, her breath catching in her lungs at the sight of him. He looked even more handsome in the jacket and tie than he did in his teaching attire, and that was saying something. A look of wonder and surprise came over his face as he stared at her.

"Hi," Annie said. "Where are you going?"

He walked forward, his eyes never leaving hers. "I'm on my way to find you."

"You are?" She smiled shyly, feeling the intensity of his attraction for her as he kept closing the distance between them. "I was on my way to find you, too."

As they spoke, Hannah faded away, discreetly heading into the open gymnasium to let them have their privacy.

"Don't mess this up," she stage-whispered to Noah as she passed him.

"I hope I haven't already done that," he replied—not to Hannah, but to Annie. His voice was as deep and solemn as his gaze. He kept approaching Annie in the empty hallway, not stopping until there was less than an arm's length between them. "I've been thinking about you every minute since I saw you last. I've missed you so much, Annie."

She bit her lower lip as emotion climbed into her throat. "I've missed you, too."

"I heard what you did—the donation that saved the prom and the clubs." He slowly shook his head. "Every time I think I know you, you do something that just...blows me away. Thank you doesn't seem sufficient, Annie. There's a gym full of high school kids in there who are having the time of their lives…because of you."

"No," she said softly. "We both did this, Noah. We did it together. And we did it with a little help from Derek, too."

"I guess that's true," he said, nodding before he sent a glance heavenward. "Thank you, Derek."

"I couldn't bear to deposit his life insurance check all this time," she admitted. "I didn't feel ready to let go of that last piece of the life I had in Dallas."

It took Noah a moment to speak. "Are you ready now?"

"Yes, I'm ready. I need to move forward and make a new life for myself."

Noah glanced down, his brows furrowed. "Annie, there's something I've wanted to tell you for a very long time. I should've had the guts to tell you the night of our prom. Instead, I hurt you with my cowardice. I'm never going to be able to forgive myself for that."

"It's all right, Noah. It was a long time ago. We were kids."

"No," he insisted, a firmness in his tone. "We were young, but we weren't children. I knew what was in my heart. I knew without any shred of doubt what I wanted for my future. *You.*"

She swallowed, staring up at him in anxious anticipation.

His frown deepened. "I should have told you that seventeen years ago. Instead of standing you up and then avoiding you for the final weeks of our senior year, I should have let you know exactly what you meant to me. You meant everything, Annie. But I didn't think I'd be able to say those words and then have the strength to let you go and pursue the dreams you had. I wanted you to be happy. I wanted to see you get the college education you'd worked so hard for all through high school, and I wanted to see you soar in your career the way I knew you would. I didn't trust that I'd be strong enough to tell you to go if I had to do it in person. I am so sorry for the way I treated you, Annie."

"I forgave you a long time ago, Noah."

He reached out to her, resting his palm against her cheek. "Now, you have this new opportunity in front of you," he said soberly. "I still want what's best for you, for your dreams, your future. When you told me about the job in Jacksonville, I told myself to be happy for you. I thought I could do the noble thing and let you go again…but I can't, Annie."

She frowned, confusion rising inside her. "What do you mean?"

"Don't go. Please, Annie. Stay here with me." He caressed her face. "I love you. I want to be with you for the rest of our lives. I want to have kids with you and grow old with you. Annie, I want it all…with you."

She couldn't believe what she was hearing. Tears prickled the backs of her eyes as her heart started pounding like a drum. "Noah, you don't—"

"I know it's unfair of me to ask you to stay," he interjected. "So, I've been thinking a lot about that, too. I can't leave Crestpoint Beach until Lainey graduates in another year and a half, but afterward I could join you in Jacksonville. And until that time, I could go see you or fly you here to see me. The point is, we can work it out. I'm willing to do whatever it takes, go to any length, in order to have you in my life forever this time. All you have to do is tell me how we can make a long-distance relationship work until we can be together."

Annie stared at him through the bleary veil of her tears. Emotion overwhelmed her. "Noah, none of those plans are going to work."

His hand slowly fell away. He inhaled deeply, then let it out in a slow sigh. "All right. I understand, Annie."

A quiet sob escaped her. "No, you don't understand. What I'm trying to tell you is that we don't have to make those kinds of plans, because I'm not taking the job after all."

"What?"

She shook her head, laughing through her tears. "I called the firm a few days ago and withdrew my acceptance. I'm staying right here in Crestpoint Beach. This is my home. It always has been. Here...with you. Noah, I can't leave you ever again. I love you. With all my heart, I love you."

"Oh, Annie." His hands came up and framed her face, drawing her to him for a sweet kiss that felt to her as if she'd been waiting for it all her life.

He murmured tender words and promises in between kisses, holding her to him like she was precious treasure.

They didn't part for long moments. When they did, Noah looked at her with new concern in his hazel eyes.

"What about your work? What about your career?"

With her arms looped around his neck, she smiled and shook her head. "Hannah and I are moving forward with the B&B plans for the beach house. We're going to do it together, and I couldn't be happier about it. We think we can be open in time for the summer tourist season."

"That's great, Annie." He kissed her again. "I've never been happier than right this moment, with you in my arms."

"Then you'd better not ever let me go again."

"No, ma'am." He rested his forehead against hers. "Unless I can persuade you to let go just long enough to come with me into the gymnasium. I think we're overdue for a slow dance."

She smiled at him, her heart bursting with joy...and love. "I thought you'd never ask."

EPILOGUE

One month later, Annie rolled out the area rug in the spacious living room of the beach house, pausing to look out the windows at the turquoise water as the high tide carried white-crested waves up to the shore. The windows were open to let in the fresh, morning air and the soothing sounds of the water. Hannah's collection of seashell wind chimes hanging on the veranda played softly in the breeze.

There was no place Annie would rather be, and she couldn't wait to be able to share her little slice of heaven with the guests she and Hannah would be welcoming once the beach house opened for its first season in a few more months. They still had a list of things to accomplish before then, including the completion of the interior furnishings and securing the town's approval to use the house as a bed-and-breakfast inn, but everything was coming together more perfectly than she ever dreamed possible.

Much like her future.

As she gazed out at the sand and surf, Noah stepped up onto the porch steps. He carried a large, flat gift the size of a pizza box under his arm. The box was wrapped in silver paper and a big red bow.

"Hey, beautiful," he called to her from the veranda when he saw her in the window.

His handsome face and the loving smile he reserved for her alone never failed to make her heart skip a beat in her chest. She hurried to the door and opened it, laughing as he immediately swept her into a one-armed embrace the instant he stepped into the house.

The past several weeks they'd spent together had been one wonderful moment after another. Annie didn't think she could love Noah more than she already had, but every day he stole another piece of her heart.

"Good morning," she said, smiling up into his warm hazel eyes. "I've missed you."

"I just saw you last night." He chuckled, kissing the tip of her nose. "But I've missed you, too. We're going to have to do something about that soon."

"Yes, I think so."

While he continued to stay at his place in town with Lainey when she was there, Annie was living on the full third floor of the beach house. The space would make an ideal owner's quarters once the house was open for business, with its own bedroom suite and full bathroom, plus a large living area overlooking the beach.

She glanced at the gift-wrapped box he was holding. "What's this?"

He held it out to her. "I realized the other day that I hadn't brought you a proper housewarming gift yet."

She tilted her head. "You didn't have to do that."

"I wanted to." He smiled tenderly, resting his palm against her cheek. "Go on, open it."

Annie carried the box to the sofa that had just arrived a few days ago and sat down to open it. Noah took a seat beside her, watching as she untied the red silk ribbon and tore off the silver paper. Setting the flat box on her lap, she carefully lifted the lid, then unfolded the tissue paper that covered the framed black-and-white photograph inside.

Her breath stopped in her lungs. "Is this what I think it is?"

"Our tree," Noah replied. "I took this photo a few days after you came back to town."

Annie stared at the old oak tree where Noah had kissed her for the very first time. The tree where they had both confessed their childhood love for each other, vowing they would always be together. It was older now, its sheltering branches fuller and heavy with leaves. The thick trunk Annie had leaned against for support while the boy she adored had kissed her so innocently stood just as stalwart as ever. Strong, despite the years.

Just like their love.

"It's beautiful, Noah. It's perfect."

"I wanted to give you something that makes you think of us when you see it. Something that not only celebrates the past we shared, but the present that reunited us, and the future we're making now…together."

Annie blinked back her happy tears. She was moved almost beyond words at the thoughtfulness of his gift, and the depth of love she saw when she looked over at him now.

"I love it, Noah. And I love you."

She set the photo beside her on the cushion and turned to wrap her arms around his neck. With her heart overflowing, she kissed him. He encircled her with his strong arms, holding her close. He felt so good, she never wanted to let go.

When Noah slowly broke their kiss, he was smiling. His eyes shone with so much devotion, it took her breath away.

"I love you, too, Annie," he said, smoothing her hair away from her cheek, his gaze locked on hers. "I loved you then, I love you now, and I will love you forever."

He eased off the sofa and went down onto one knee in front of her.

Annie stared at him, her heartbeat accelerating. "Noah, what are you doing?"

His gaze rooted on hers, he gently took her left hand between his palms. "I have known from the moment I first laid eyes on you in Mrs. Dennis's third grade class that you were the girl for me, Annie. You've been my best friend, my confidant, my safe harbor, my only love…and you still are. You always will be."

She bit her lip, struggling to keep her emotions at bay as she absorbed the beauty of his words. She could hardly breathe as she watched him reach into the front pocket of his slacks to withdraw a small red box. He opened it, revealing a sparkling diamond ring.

"I love you, Annie Taylor. I need you, and I never want to know another day without you at my side." He took the ring out of the box and held it in his fingers. A nervous smile broke over his handsome face. "I don't want to rush you, or ask you to make a decision before you're ready for it, but I want you to know that I'm ready. My heart is yours forever. So, what do you say, Annie? Will you marry me?"

"Noah…" She swallowed, tears clogging her throat and her vision. "Yes."

"Yes?" He beamed at her, those twin dimples pushing her heart right over the edge.

Annie nodded vigorously. "Yes, Noah Davis. I love you with all my heart, and I would love to be your wife."

He took her hand and slipped the ring onto her finger. Then he rose to his feet, drawing her up with him and into his arms. He kissed her again, and Annie smiled against his lips, unable to contain her happiness as they held each other.

What they had in the past was beautiful and intense. They would have those memories for a lifetime, plus all of the new memories they were already creating together. Perhaps, in time, they would add more than memories to the family they had become.

Neither time nor distance had been enough to take away what they felt for each other.

And now, after being apart for so long, they had been given another chance, a second chance, at love.

* * *

THANK you so much for joining Annie and Noah on the journey to their happily-ever-after. I hope you loved this first visit to Crestpoint Beach and the start of the Turning Tides series!

If you enjoyed **Back to You**, please let me know by sharing your review for the book on Amazon, Goodreads, or BookBub.

Are you ready for the next book in the series? You can order **Meant to Be** now!

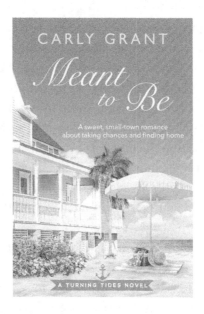

Hannah Taylor is spontaneous and fun. Building contractor Gabe Lawson is all business, a handsome newcomer to Crestpoint Beach who's looking for a fresh start. When Hannah and her sister hire Gabe to help get their beach house B&B inspection-ready ahead of the summer tourist season, sparks fly between these total opposites.

But there's more to both of them than meets the eye, and soon free-spirited Hannah and "measure twice, cut once" Gabe are fighting deeper feelings for each other. When a setback threatens to pull them apart, can Hannah and Gabe turn their "opposites attract" romance into happily-ever-after?

WANT A CHANCE TO WIN A SIGNED BOOK?

JOIN MY READER LIST

Be sure to join my private email list at CarlyGrant.com to get updates on my new and upcoming books. Each month, active subscribers have a chance to win a signed copy of Back to You!

I'll also let you know about special sales and promotions, exclusive content, and more.

ABOUT THE AUTHOR

Carly Grant loves Hallmark movies, small-town life, sandy beaches, kittens, and cupcakes--not necessarily in that order. She lives in her hometown in Florida with her husband, where she spends her days soaking up the sunshine and dreaming up sweet romances and happily-ever-afters.

Visit CarlyGrant.com for book info and more!

facebook.com/CarlyGrantAuthor
bookbub.com/profile/carly-grant
goodreads.com/carlygrantauthor